The Sea Captain and the Lady

By Vada Foster

D1738247

THE SEA CAPTAIN AND THE LADY
© 2008 BY VADA FOSTER

ISBN 10: 1-933113-89-8
ISBN 13: 978-1-933113-89-0

First Printing: 2008

This Trade Paperback Is Published By
Intaglio Publications
Walker, LA USA
WWW.INTAGLIOPUB.COM

This is a work of fiction. Names, characters, places, and incidents are the product of the author's imagination or are used fictitiously, and any resemblance to actual persons, living or dead, businesses, companies, events, or locales is entirely coincidental.

CREDITS
EXECUTIVE EDITOR: VERDA FOSTER
ILLUSTRATIONS BY CHRISTINE DAVID AND KAZ WILLIAMS
COVER DESIGN BY POLLY ROBINSON

Dedication

This one, and all the rest I write, is for my partner Gypsy.
She is my muse, my motivation and a constant source of
Gypsy magic. I love you always.

Acknowledgements

A whole heap of people helped me along in way in turning my short story into a novel. Carolyn Veiga and Bea Bastien provided a never ending supply of pirate T-shirts for inspiration and Carolyn also read an early draft, offering helpful suggestions. Lori Buck gave me much editorial assistance. Lori Lake and Jennifer Fulton provided guidance and encouragement, for which I am heartily grateful. My sister Verda accepted the task of editing the final manuscript and put a gun to my head about a few things she wanted changed. Sheri Payton took a chance on me without question. My "Mom" Jeannine Pomerleau spent numerous days babysitting for our animals to free me up to write, and I love her for it. Valerie Hayken did the first version of the cover, and Polly Robinson did the final version. Chrissy David created drawings for the book that brought the characters to life. Most of all, I have to say thank you to Gypsy who gave me all the encouragement in the world, and made it possible for me to take the time to write.

Disclaimer

History buffs and students of Pirate-ology will know that I have taken several liberties with the characters Mary Read, Anne Bonny, and Jack Rackham. I tried to be as true to their histories as possible within the confines of my story, but those women had other ideas about what they wanted to do. The epidemic I described did not happen, but the collapse of the bell tower in Elgin Cathedral did. So please if you're looking for a whole lot of historical accuracy, you will need to look elsewhere. I hope, however, you will find it's a hell of a yarn.

Colleen

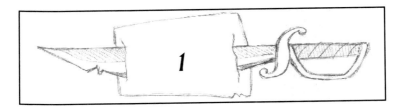

Hartlepool, England, 1709

Colleen Edwards inspected the embroidery on the linen napkin she had just finished. Not as good as her mother's work, but she thought mum would find it passable. The sound of a harness jingling, indicating her family was returning home, brought her to her feet. She glanced out the window and saw the wagon approaching, but rather than stopping in front of the door to allow her mother to alight, as was Charles habit, the horses continued toward the barn. Odd, she thought. Perhaps her brother dozed off as he drove home. Taking her shawl from the peg by the door, she drew it around her shoulders, more for propriety's sake than because it had cooled down. She strode toward the barn and saw the team stopped just outside the structure. Only one of the doors was open, and the entrance was not wide enough to accommodate the wagon. As she got closer, she could see her older brother Charles leaning so far forward in his seat it was a miracle he did not topple into the traces. By all appearances, he truly had fallen asleep on the way home. Her mother also sat slumped in her seat, and young Thomas was sprawled out in the back of the wagon, still as the sack of flour against which he rested.

"Wake up, Charles! You need to move the wagon closer to the pantry, or I'll not be helping you carry all those heavy..." Her voice trailed off when Charles turned his head slowly toward her, as if the muscles refused to obey his commands. His eyes were red and swollen, and his skin was pasty white.

"Sorry, Col. I seem to have ... no energy, could not even rein in the horses. I'll fetch the wagon up to the house later when I feel better." The reins dropped from his limp fingers, and he gingerly climbed down from the seat. Almost immediately, he was seized with a fit of stomach cramps, and he emptied the contents of his stomach mere inches from where Colleen stood.

"Oh, Charles, let me help you..." He shook his head feebly and nodded toward their mother, who was still slumped over in the seat.

"I'll be all right, Col. But Mum has been awful still most of the way back from town. I think she'll need some help. And Thomas is quieter than I ever knew him to be. Maybe you could look out for them, 'eh? I'll unharness the—" Another cramp took hold of him, this one making him feel as if he must evacuate his bowels. He turned and ran for the privy, leaving Colleen staring after him.

Shaking her head at her brother's odd behavior, Colleen walked to the far side of the wagon and took her mother's hand. It had all the warmth and animation of a dead flounder. "Mum, I've come to help you down. Give us your other hand, as well." Betsy Ann seemed to perk up when she heard Colleen's voice. She turned and smiled wanly at her and placed her left hand on Colleen's shoulder.

"Thank you, dear. It seems some sort of malady has struck us all since dining at your Aunt Margaret's house. We must have stopped a dozen times on the way home to—"

"I think I know," Colleen said with a distasteful look on her face as she helped her mother from the wagon. Betsy Ann wobbled a bit but grabbed the edge of the wagon to steady herself. Colleen took her elbow to guide her toward the house, but Betsy Ann attempted to veer toward the bed of the wagon where her youngest son lay so unnaturally quiet. Colleen put her back on course. "Never mind, Mum, I'll come back for Thomas. Let's get you into bed." Betsy Ann did not have the strength to argue. She simply nodded and allowed Colleen to support her as she slowly made her way into the house.

When Colleen was certain her mother was comfortably in bed, she turned and went back to the barn. Charles had yet to release the horses from their harness, so she freed them, knowing they would head straight to their stalls looking for something to eat. "I'll come back and brush you in a bit, if my lazy brother does not," she promised the horses, and true to their natures, they each made their way to their stalls and began to forage for scraps of hay. Colleen did not want to take the time to climb into the loft for hay, but she scooped a handful of grain up for each animal and spread it in the feed troughs in each stall, then she quickly returned to where Thomas was still sprawled in the back of the wagon. Colleen heard a soft moan as she approached, followed by the sounds of retching. Feeling her own stomach turn she swallowed and took a deep breath, praying she would not do the same. She stepped up onto the running board and saw Thomas lying on his side doubled up with painful cramps.

"Oh, Tommy lad, what has happened to still your youthful spirit and bring you such pain?" She reached over the side of the wagon and gathered the limp form into her arms, heedless of the stench of vomit and feces clinging to his clothing.

She straightened up and took a deep breath, marching resolutely toward the house with Thomas clutched against her.

Nudging the door open with her hip, she made her way to Thomas's bed, laying him gently on the straw mattress. His eyelids fluttered open briefly, and he looked into Colleen's face. His cheeks were flushed, whether from embarrassment over losing control of his bowels or because he was as hot as a burning coal, Colleen didn't know. "Sorry, Col," he said, his voice raspy and faint. "I've soiled meself."

She kissed his forehead and smiled "'Tis not the worst thing you've done, laddie. Now let's get you out of these clothes before we both faint from the stench." She pulled his shirt over his head, careful to avoid rubbing his face in the mess there. Her own stomach turned over at the smell; she had never done well with sickness, and even the hint of it was enough to send her dashing to the privy. But knowing she was the only one to care for her family, she managed to keep her gorge from rising and continued to strip the small boy. She tossed the offensive garments out the front door, figuring she would deal with them after she'd seen to all of her sick people. She failed to notice Charles walking up from the back house until she saw the soiled clothing in a heap at his feet.

"Pelting me with ruined knickers, Col? A bit of getting even for me losing me supper on you, is it?" He smiled, but the smudges under his eyes effectively prevented the smile from going any higher than his lips. Colleen shivered at the expression on his face. He had gone from a vibrant, healthy-looking young man to a gaunt old man in the course of a day.

"Aye, and you're lucky that's not all I do to you. You nearly caused me to lose my griddlecakes, big brother. Get in the house, will you, and get out of those horrible clothes. I'll be in to see to you shortly."

Whatever illness they had contracted, it frightened her more than she would admit to herself. She had no idea what to do, other than try to keep them comfortable and hope it was something that would soon pass. It was too late to go into town for the doctor, but she vowed that if they were not better by morning, she would fetch help.

"Aye, Cap'n," he said with a halfhearted grin, turning and staggering through the door. Colleen shook her head as she watched him go. It was going to be a long night.

Drawing a bucket of water from the well, Colleen went to the bedside of each of them in turn, giving them sips of the cool liquid. But none of them could keep the water down for more than a few minutes, and after awhile, they refused to even attempt to drink, knowing the cramping would soon follow. They had all been seized with bouts of diarrhea, and Colleen had long since run out of linen to change their bedding and had simply laid fresh straw under them.

Evening turned into night, then to morning, and still Colleen trudged from one bedside to the next, trying to comfort when clearly there was nothing she could do. Exhausted from her own pain-filled day, and the fear she felt for her family, she finally allowed herself to sit—for just a moment, she vowed—to rest and get her strength back so she could care for them. She was jolted from a dream in which her father appeared as the bowsprit on the front of his ship, where normally the likeness of her mother guided the vessel over the seas. The ship came closer to shore, speeding toward the wooden pilings of the pier in Hartlepool. The wooden carving of her father spoke to her even as the ship rammed into the piling, splintering into small pieces. "Take care of yourself, Col. There's no hope for me...." And then the bowsprit once again had the face of her mother, as it crumbled and fell beneath the waves.

Sweating and gasping, Colleen sat up in her mother's chair, looking around the room as if to orient herself. Daylight was filtering through the casements, and she could make out Thomas's form on his pallet, still and pale in the early morning gloom. With a groan, she rose from her chair and went to her brother's side, thinking he might now be ready to hold down a bit of water. She knelt to lift his head for a drink and it lolled off to one side, limp. She brushed the hair from his forehead to place her lips there to see if he was still hot, but his skin was cool, his body lifeless. Unable to believe her own senses, she picked up his hand and chafed his wrist briskly, trying to work some warmth into him. After several minutes, she heard a sound both strange and foreign to her ears, then realized it was coming from deep inside her. Tears splashed on the precious face of her little brother, and she pulled him into her arms, rocking and clutching him as if this could bring him back.

"Tommy, stop teasing me please. I can't bear it. Open your eyes, little one. I'll let you have the sling Father made for me. Anything I have is yours, only open your eyes."

She had no idea how long she sat on the floor with her brother cradled in her arms, but the sun was high and the heat was rising. It promised to be another scorching hot day. Colleen finally laid him down again on his pallet, and kissing his forehead, covered him with her shawl. She stumbled out to the pump and drew another bucket of water, scooping handfuls of it to dash on her face to try to reduce the swelling and redness in her eyes. Gulping in several draughts of air, she turned to go back into the house and see how her mother and Charles fared. She would not tell them about Thomas, fearing it might cause their own conditions to worsen, so she tried to put on a brave face as she opened the door to her mother's room.

The eyes Betsy Ann turned on her were dull and lifeless, her lips dry and cracked, her cheeks sunken. She made an effort to smile, but the drawn look on her face frightened Colleen so much she very nearly bolted from the room. Betsy Ann lifted her hand slightly from the bed and beckoned for Colleen to come closer.

"Here's my Beanpole. I've been wondering whether you were going to lie abed this live long day. How are the boys?" Her mother's voice was reedy and thin, and Colleen had to kneel by the bed to hear her.

"I've not seen Charles yet this morning. Thomas is ... not in pain, Mum."

"Ah, he's well then?" Colleen averted her eyes from her mother's and nodded, unable to bring the lie to her lips. Betsy Ann sighed, her eyes closed, and she seemed to sink in upon herself. Fearing her mother too had died, Colleen clutched at her hand, and the faint pressure she received in return reassured her.

"I must go into town and fetch the doctor," Colleen said, laying a kiss upon her mother's cheek. Colleen felt helpless in the face of whatever had sickened her family. Nothing she tried to do was of any help to them. She was not willing to risk the lives of her mother and remaining brother by trusting to God, as she was certain her mother would have wished.

"Not ... necessary.... We've just had a bit of ... bad fish. We—"

"Mother ... please, there is nothing I can do for you. I need help. Surely you can see that. I promise, I'll be so quick, you'll not even know I've gone. Here, have a sip of water, won't you? Your lips are so dry...."

"Rub a bit on my lips then, dear. I shan't be able to keep anything down ... my stomach ... hurts so much."

Doing as she was bid, Colleen dipped a clean handkerchief in

6

the water bucket and put it against her mother's lips. Her mother shook her head after a few moments to indicate she no longer wanted the cloth against her mouth, and Colleen removed it, dipped it in the bucket again and placed the cool cloth against her forehead.

Unable to do anything more for her mother, she rose to her feet and picked up the bucket. "I'm going to check on Charles, then head to town. I'll be back soon." Betsy Ann gave a slight nod to show she heard, and Colleen interpreted the motion as permission to leave.

Charles was slightly more alert than Betsy Ann but did not have enough energy to rise from the soiled straw upon which he lay. His lips were dry and bleeding, his cheeks gaunt and sunken. It seemed her brother and her mother had aged fifty years overnight. Colleen tried to put on a brave face before she walked over to his bed, but she could not mask the fear and sadness from him. They were closer than any other pair of brothers and sisters she knew, and he read her emotions as she approached.

"My God, Colleen ... has someone died? Is it Mother?"

"No ... not Mother...." Her voice broke, and she sobbed as she dropped to her knees by his bed, her head resting on his hollow chest. She felt the heaving of his chest as he began to cry, and she clutched him tightly. He brushed his hand over her hair with all the strength of a butterfly's wing before his hand dropped limply to his side. Colleen lifted her head to look into his ashen face and knew if she did not get help, and soon, the rest of the family would be dead, as well.

"I've no idea what to do for you, Charles. I'm going into town to see if I can fetch the doctor back to have a look at you. Please..." Her voice trailed off as she realized she had no idea what, if anything, she might say that could give her brother hope. Charles gave a weak nod and attempted a smile, but almost immediately was seized with dry heaves. There was nothing more in his stomach to bring up.

When Charles's head dropped forward and he fell asleep, Colleen walked to the trunk at the foot of his bed and pulled out some of his old trousers that were now far too short for him. He'd taught her to ride astride a horse years earlier, and she had learned then how practical it was to wear trousers on horseback. And because she wanted to complete her task as quickly as possible, she decided not to use the carriage that would force her to remain on the roads. On horseback, she could make the trip to town in half the time.

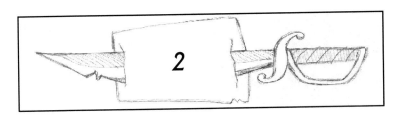

The streets of Hartlepool were quiet and deserted when Colleen dismounted in the yard in front of the doctor's house. Before she could raise her hand to knock, the door opened to reveal the haggard face of the doctor's wife. The woman's eyes widened as she took in the attire of the girl who stood wide-eyed and frantic on her porch.

Before Colleen could draw a breath to say why she'd come, Mrs. Gable shook her head and said, "If you've come for my husband, I fear you've a long wait. He's been out since last evening. Seems the town has got some sort of plague. Ten dead already by the last count, and that was several hours ago when he stopped home for some clean clothes. Say, aren't you Betsy Ann Edwards's daughter?" Colleen nodded, and the woman smiled. "She's a fine hand for sewing, and that's a fact. I have two of her—"

"Please, Mrs. Gable, my mother is ill and my brother, as well. My baby brother is..." She choked on the words, unable to finish, but the look on Mrs. Gable's face told her she knew. Gulping in a breath of air, she pleaded, "Can you tell me where I might find your husband? I need—"

"I'm sorry, child, but the last place he visited was your aunt and uncle's house. They ... er, well, I'm sorry, dear. They're both dead. This is a horrible thing, horrible. Why I—"

"Where was he going next?" Colleen interrupted, determined to get some help for her family before they met the same fate as her aunt and uncle.

"Oh, well, it was to the Mitchell's house, over by the chemist's shop. But he may have gone—"

"Thank you, Mrs. Gable. I'll find him." She turned and sprinted to where her horse was cropping grass and vaulted onto the animal's back.

Mrs. Gable looked after her sadly, knowing there was little chance her family would be alive when she returned home. "A shame," she muttered. "Such a lovely girl, but how odd she looks in trousers."

Colleen finally caught up with the exhausted doctor at the home of the cobbler. He had left the house and was heading for his wagon when she wheeled her horse up in front of him. His clothes reeked of the smells of human waste, and his grim face showed he had not had much—if any—luck with the people who had been stricken with whatever it was that had affected her family.

"Good God, boy! You gave me a fright, galloping right up on top of me like that. Why, I might have..." He stopped as he realized the rider was not a boy, and he tried to call to mind the name of the young lady whom he had undoubtedly delivered into the world. "Colleen, is that you? What in the world are you doing in boy's clothing?"

"Dr. Gable, please, you have to come with me. Mother and Charles ... they ... they..." Her voice began to quiver, and the doctor knew she was very nearly hysterical.

"There, there, come and sit down and tell me—"

"There's no time! Please. Thomas is dead, and I can't help them!" Tears coursed down her cheeks as she pleaded with him to help her.

"Were they in town yesterday?" She nodded, and his face looked even more grim. "Did they buy fish from the fish stall at the market? That seems to be the common link with all the people who have taken ill. I've never seen it myself, but from the symptoms, I suspect it may be cholera. From what I've read, it can be contracted from contaminated fish and is nearly always fatal."

"I have no idea. I wasn't with them. They ate with Aunt Margaret, I know.... Oh, God, your wife told me they're dead also! Doctor, you have to come with me.... I can't bear to lose my family."

"Child, there's nothing I can do. These poor folks are losing every bit of moisture in their bodies as if they're dying of thirst. I can't get them to keep anything down. If you can get your mother and brother to drink something and not vomit it back up, they may live. I have no experience to help me deal with this type of thing."

"Surely there must be some medicine ... or you could bleed them to remove the poison," the frantic girl cried, clutching at his sleeve.

"Colleen, I wish I could help you. Truly, I can't. Last night, I went from one home to the next, watching most of the people die and helpless to prevent it. I have told you all I know to do. Try giving them some weak tea, that has helped one or two who did not seem to be as ill. Not all have died. Perhaps your family will make it. But it is crucial you get something in them soon. It may already be too late. Hurry home, lass."

Colleen stood for a moment, unable to believe there was nothing the doctor could do to help. When he picked up his bag and climbed into his wagon, she looked at him hopefully, but he shook his head and slapped the reins against the horse's flanks.

Colleen watched the dust rising from the wagon wheel ruts for a moment, then drew a determined breath, mounted her horse, and nudged her into a gallop toward home.

The house was deathly silent when she pushed open the door. Dust motes swirled in the light that followed her into the dim room. She had fetched a bucket of fresh water on the way to the house and laid a fire in the cook stove to boil water for tea. While the stove was heating, she went to her mother's room, opening the door a crack and listening for the sound of breathing. The faint breath she could hear gave her hope. She returned to the kitchen to put the kettle on the flames, then crossed to her brother's room. Silence greeted her when she opened his door. Her heart pounded with the dread of what she would find. She softly called his name but heard no response.

"Charles, it's Colleen. I've put some water on to boil for tea. The doctor said you must keep some liquid down if you hope to..." She stopped in mid-sentence when she reached his bedside and could tell from the absolute stillness of his chest he no longer breathed. His unseeing eyes were fixed on the window where he must have watched for her return as his life ebbed. "No!" Colleen dropped to her knees and pulled his lifeless form into her arms. She stifled the sobs rising in her throat to avoid alarming her mother through the thin wall that separated the two rooms.

Colleen had no idea how much time had passed as she sat with her brother in her arms, but she feared it was long enough for the water on the stove to have boiled away. With a sigh, she closed his eyelids and lightly kissed his forehead. She lay him on the floor unable to bear the thought of returning him to his soiled bed. "If there be a God, may He give you peace, dear brother," she whispered.

Just enough water remained in the pan to fill the teapot, so Colleen added tea to the pot and set it to brewing while she prepared a tray. Dreading what she might find in her mother's room and knowing she must ultimately tell her about the loss of her family, her feet dragged as she crossed the room.

"Mum?" she called out softly and heard a moan from her mother in reply. Heartened to know she still lived, she crossed to her bedside a bit livelier than she had entered the room and put the tray on the night table. "I've brought you a bit of tea, Mum. The doctor says you must drink something."

"Oh, thank you, dear, but I fear I would not..." Her voice lowered to the point where Colleen could not hear without leaning down close to her. When she did, she felt the heat radiating off her mother's body and perceived the smell of death clinging to her as certainly as it had to her brothers. "...keep it down," she finished in a whisper.

"Please, try to take some tea. It's our only hope. I beg you, please try."

"All right, Beanpole, perhaps a bit of tea." Colleen placed the cup of weak tea against her mother's lips and allowed just a few drops at a time to trickle into her mouth. Within minutes, the poor woman began to heave and the tiny bit of liquid she had consumed was expelled. With what strength she still possessed, she shook her head and pushed the cup away. "I can't bear it, perhaps in a while." Closing her eyes, she lay back on the bed. Her breath was shallow and foul.

Not knowing what else she might do, Colleen lay beside her mother and pulled her head onto her chest as Betsy Ann had done for her when she was a child. It always comforted her, and when she woke, she was feeling better, whatever the problem. She stroked her hair and hummed a lullaby until her mother fell asleep, her breathing even and rhythmic. "Please, Mum, stay with me," she whispered. "I don't think I can take it if I lose you, as well. I love you."

The words roused Betsy Ann, and she whispered, "I love you," in return, then with a sigh, she was gone.

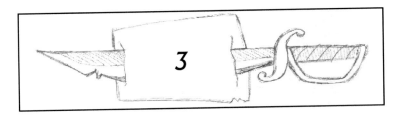

Colleen stood on the wharf watching as the *Betsy Ann* made its way into the slip reserved for her father's use when he was in home port. She had made the trip into town every day for the past four weeks, knowing her father was due to return soon and not wishing for him to learn the news from anyone but herself. Other than the doctor who knew only that Thomas was dead, no one in the city knew her mother and brothers were gone. The doctor may have surmised about the others, but she did not confirm his suspicions.

Charles Edwards Sr. waved from the prow of the ship and tossed a rope to the wharf-hand standing by, as the crew took care of the business of making the ship secure in her berth. As soon as the gangplank made contact with the wharf, Colleen was aboard ship. She threw herself into her father's arms and hugged him as if it had been years since she'd seen him, instead of months. Tears came unbidden to her eyes and stained the red jacket he wore, and after a moment, her father gently pushed her to arm's length.

"What's this, Col?" He wiped the tears from her cheeks with his thumbs and kissed her on the forehead. He scanned the wharf and surrounding buildings searching for the rest of his family. "Where's your mum and brothers then? Should you be out on your own?"

"Oh, Father, they're gone. All of them. There was an epidemic, and I stayed home because I was not feeling well. I should have been with them, I might have saved them. It's my fault. Please forgive me, Father." Her words were punctuated with hiccups and were all but unintelligible. Tears poured unchecked from her reddened eyes and left tracks in the dust that had settled on her cheeks during the trip from home.

Alarmed, Charles grasped Colleen's shoulders and stared into her stricken face. "Colleen, slow down. I can't understand you. An epidemic you say?"

"Yes. The doctor said there was nothing he could do. Mum, Charles, and Thomas dined with Auntie Margaret and Uncle Edgar. There was something wrong with the fish…"

Charles finally grasped the meaning of her words, and the color drained from his face. Colleen took his arm and guided him to an overturned dinghy. "Sit down, Father. You look as if you might faint." She continued to hold his arm as he lowered himself onto the little boat. He sucked in several deep breaths in an effort to stave off the tears threatening to fall, but there was no holding back the grief. He buried his face in his hands and sobbed, which shocked Colleen. She had never in her life seen a tear in his eye, and certainly nothing like the great sobs wracking his body now. She sat beside him and drew his head to her shoulder. He seemed to have no will of his own and simply stayed where she put him, the tears continuing to fall unchecked. Not knowing what to do or say to alleviate his pain, Colleen held him until he quieted, her hands moving up and down his back in what she hoped was a soothing motion. Suddenly, she remembered her mother holding her in just the same way when she was a child, and she very nearly dissolved in tears herself. She took a deep breath and sat up straight, determined to be strong for her father.

It seemed as if hours had passed as the two sat, not speaking, both staring at the rolling waves of the North Sea, but in fact it was only a few minutes. The sailors had efficiently secured the *Betsy Ann*, and James Henry, the first mate, was looking to her father for directions.

"Dismiss the men, Mr. Henry. Have them back by morning to unload the cargo. I'll settle up their wages then."

"Aye, Cap'n. But I fear some of them might need a wee bit of money before morning for ... lodging, and the like. I could..."

Charles sighed and rose to his feet. "Of course, you're right." He loosened the collar of his shirt and from around his neck pulled out a chain bearing a single key. He handed the key to James. "Five Crowns each should keep them until the morrow, I vow. I will make a proper settlement with each of them then. I ... have had more than a bit of bad news, Mr. Henry. Forgive me, but I am going to take Colleen home now. Thank you for taking care of this for me."

"Oh, aye, 'tis no worry, Cap'n, I'll take care of the ship and the men." He cut his eyes toward Colleen as if to inquire about what news she had shared with the captain, but Colleen shook her head. She mouthed the word "tomorrow" to him as she linked arms with her father and led him off the ship.

Charles was silent all the way home. He allowed Colleen to drive the horse cart, which was something he would normally not do. It was not until they pulled into the cobblestone drive leading to the house that he turned to Colleen and asked, "Where ... where are they?"

"Near the old orchard. Mum loved it there in the spring when the blossoms covered the trees, remember? She took me there often when I was small. I thought ... it would be a peaceful place for them." Her voice thickened with emotion and tears once again pooled in her eyes. She scrubbed her face impatiently as if to will them away.

"That sounds lovely. Yes, she did love it there." Colleen brought the cart to a stop in front of the barn, and Charles climbed down from his seat. He stepped around and held his hand up to assist her and saw for the first time the impact the past month had had on Colleen. Her eyes were sunken, her cheeks hollow. She had obviously lost considerable weight judging by the way her dress billowed around her slender frame. He gathered her into his arms and hugged her tightly. "Oh, Colleen, how very hard it must have been for you to ... to have to deal with ... all this alone. I'm so sorry, my dear. Come into the house and let me fix you some tea."

"Father, I must see to the horse. Please, go and rest for a while, and when I come back, I shall make you some tea. And later, if you wish, I'll take you to ... the spot where they're resting."

Charles rose the morning after he had returned home and forced down a few bites of the breakfast Colleen prepared for him, then, without speaking at all, he went back to his room and climbed into bed. Colleen could not help but remember the way she felt in the days after the loss of her family and knew it was probably best to leave him alone to grieve. Late that afternoon, while Colleen was preparing supper, she heard the sound of a harness jingling and went outside to find Mr. Henry pulling up in a wagon with its cargo covered by canvas sheets. She waved in greeting and smiled at the old seaman, who was also her father's closest friend. If anybody could reach her father, it would be Mr. Henry.

Mr. Henry vaulted over the side of the wagon and enveloped Colleen in a hug. When he released her to look into her face, the smile with which she first greeted him evaporated, replaced with a look of grief that was plain to see. "Oh, lass, 'tis sad I am to learn of what happened here while we were away. The doctor could not tell me if any of yer family survived..."

"None but I, Mr. Henry, and I would gladly have given up my life to spare theirs if the choice were mine to make."

"Oh no, child, yer mother would hate to hear ye talking like that. She would want ye to be there for yer father. The truth of it is, yer the strongest one in the family." When Colleen grimaced and shook her head, Mr. Henry put his arm around her shoulder and pulled her close to him again. "'Tis true, lass. And yer father will need that strength in the time to come. Give us a smile now and help me make a decision about these stones." He began to remove the canvas from the wagon, and she stood watching with a look of curiosity on her face.

"Stones? I don't understand how I–" She stopped mid-sentence as the cargo was revealed. There were a half-dozen pieces of marble in various sizes and colors, all of them with one side and the bottom flat so they could ride in the wagon without tipping. "Mr. Henry, are these marble?" When he nodded, she came closer to the wagon and touched the cool stones. "These are truly beautiful. Where did you come by them?"

"Did yer father not tell ye how we came to be acquainted?"

"He said you carved the bowsprit for his ship and became friends after that. I was very young and really don't remember much."

"Well, that's true enough, but in fact, when I met yer father, I was a stone-cutter. A good one, too, before I took to drinkin'. I was well on the way to killin' myself when yer father sat next to me in a pub and started talkin'. Before I knew it, he had me sobered up and carvin' that wooden image of yer mother. I couldn't just give that beautiful piece of work to someone else to put on the ship, so I hired on to help build the *Betsy Ann*. By the time she was finished, I was through with drinkin', and yer father asked me to sign on with him as first mate. Before I left Hartlepool, I stored me stones and tools with me cousin and asked him to keep 'em safe until I needed 'em. Well, I reckon I need some now, and I'd be grateful if ye could help decide which stones should be used and how ye want them to read."

Colleen's eyes were drawn to a white marble stone shot through with tiny streaks of silver. "This is a magnificent stone, Mr. Henry. I think my mother would love it if she were here."

"'Tis a fine choice, lass. This piece of marble comes from the same quarry in Italy where the stone Michelangelo used to make his beautiful *David* came from."

"Truly? Then it must be Mother's. She told me how taken she was with his work when she went to Italy with my father..." Her voice trailed off, and she swallowed hard a few times to blink back tears. Taking a deep breath, she studied the remaining stones carefully and selected two more for her brothers. "I think we should ask Father what he would like to have on the stones. If you would like to water your horses, there's a trough over there. Come into the house when you're through and we'll ask him. I'll see if he's up to receiving visitors."

19

Charles was non-responsive when Colleen knocked on his door, so she opened it and went into the room. He was still in his nightshirt, sitting up in bed, eyes wide open but unseeing. His gaze flicked briefly to Colleen before returning to a spot on the wall.

"Father, Mr. Henry has come to see you. He brought some beautiful stones to—"

"No. I don't want to talk about that now. Perhaps in a few days. Tell him I said thank you for his kindness. I can't..." His eyes looked almost wild for a moment, then he retreated back into the same morose silence in which she found him. Colleen crossed to her father's bed and patted his shoulder. He placed his hand over hers for a moment, then let it fall back to the bed.

"Don't be anxious, Father. I'll ask him to come back. Rest now and I'll bring your tea in a little while."

"Yes" was all he said as she backed quietly out of the room.

Mr. Henry unloaded the stones Colleen had chosen and placed them in the barn. He was making his way toward the house when Colleen came out with a look of anguish on her face.

"He said to thank you and tell you he's not ready to deal with this just yet. He asked if you could come back in a few days. Oh, Mr. Henry, he looks so—hollow. I don't know what to do for him."

Mr. Henry put his arm around her shoulders and gave her a brief squeeze. "He'll come around, Col. We don't need to make a decision today on the engraving for the stones. When I come back in a day or so, I'll start working on them, if that's all right with ye."

"Yes, of course, that would be fine. And if he's not prepared to make a decision about what should go on the stones, I'm sure you and I could come up with something appropriate."

"Indeed we can, lass." They walked toward the wagon in silence and Mr. Henry climbed up in the seat. "Get word to me if you need me for anything before I get back out here again." Colleen nodded and Mr. Henry smiled and kissed her forehead.

"That's me girl. I'll see ye soon." He clucked at the horses and laid the reins across their necks.

Colleen waved as the wagon pulled away, then with a sigh, she went back into the house to make tea.

For several days, Colleen prepared meals for her father and brought them to him, but he refused to answer her knock at his door. The full chamber pot left outside his door on several occasions was the only indication he was even in the room. When he stopped even setting the chamber pot outside the door, Colleen knew she must ignore the fact of the closed door and go in to help him.

She was alarmed by what she saw when she entered the room after a tentative knock. Her father sat in the chair where her mother spent many hours sewing and embroidering. He had Betsy Ann's shawl draped over his shoulders, the ends clutched together over his chest. His face was gaunt under a growth of stubble, his eyes sunken and hollow. Colleen could not stifle a gasp of surprise at his appearance, and the noise caused him to glance her way.

"This was her favorite shawl, Colleen. I brought the yarn from India for her, and she spent weeks working to get the pattern just right. So colorful it was ... she looked beautiful wearing it, eh, lass? You were just a wee girl then, and Thomas just beginning to grow in her belly. Gone. All gone." He attempted to smile, but it was more of a grimace. Tears gathered in his lower eyelids, then dropped unnoticed to his lap.

Colleen could not think of what to do to draw her father out of his misery. She crossed the room and stood before him, her hands held out to him. He took her small hands in his calloused ones and rather than allowing her to pull him up, which was her intention, he drew her down onto his lap. She buried her face in the crook of his neck and breathed in the scent she associated with her father from her earliest memories of him. Those memories conjured an image of her mother by his side, and at that, tears coursed down her cheeks. She tightened her grip around his waist as if fearful of losing him, as well. Charles brushed the tears away with his thumbs and held her tightly to his breast. Colleen was exhausted from the emotional and physical toll the past weeks had taken on her. Without meaning to, she dropped into a light sleep while her father gently rocked her. Whether it was the realization he still had a daughter who needed him or that the grief had retreated to a manageable place within him, after Colleen woke up, Charles asked her to bring him some hot water so he might clean himself and take a meal with her. She kissed his cheek and went to put water on to boil, her spirits lightened for the first time since the wagon drew to a stop in front of the barn with her nearly dead brother at the reins.

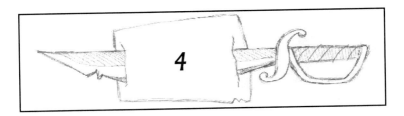

Durham, England 1711

"Oh, Father, please. I can't bear another day in this dreary place. You know I already speak French as well as the instructor, and my English and sums are top drawer. It's agony for me to be locked up with these simpering ninnies, who day in and day out speak only about the blokes they fancy and the children they'll bear them. Ugh. I shall go mad if you don't take me with you to sea where the air is fresh and there are no simpering—"

"Come now, Col," Charles interrupted. "Surely it can't be as bad as all that. This is the finest finishing school for ladies in northern England. Here you are safe, well cared for—"

"And bored beyond measure, Father. I have endured nearly two years in this ghastly dungeon. I am a woman and old enough to make my own choices. I tell you, if you do not take me with you, I shall leave here of my own accord."

This was not a new argument. Each time Charles was able to take time between voyages to visit Colleen in Durham, she begged to be allowed to accompany him, and each time he refused, believing she was better off in school than on the sea. He firmly believed the sailor's life was not for a woman. But it was obvious she was miserable, and truth be told, he missed her terribly, for he only saw her two or three times a year. He saw in her eyes that she'd reached her limit, and the thought of her actually leaving the place and being lost to him forever was not something he could live with. Colleen was like Betsy Ann in many ways, and Charles had never been able to say no to her either when it really mattered.

"Well, perhaps we could give it a try—" Colleen launched herself at his chest, wrapping her arms around his neck and raining kisses on his cheek. "A try, mind you. I'm not saying—"

"Oh, Father, thank you! You'll not regret it, I promise. I shall work harder than any man aboard, you'll see."

Her eyes sparkled with a life Charles had not seen in many years. Despite his initial misgivings, he thought perhaps it would be the best thing for her after all. Colleen was not the fragile flower her mother had been. She'd worked shoulder to shoulder with Charles when the old homestead was producing crops for the market in Hartlepool, lifting and carrying the same load as he. And a blind man could see her spirit was being crushed within the walls of the school. "Go fetch your things then, while I discuss this with the headmistress." No other encouragement was needed. Colleen lifted her skirts and vaulted up the stairs to the small room she shared with three other girls. Charles could not help but laugh at her antics as he went in search of the headmistress.

Colleen insisted she be part of the crew of the *Betsy Ann* and not simply a passenger. When she first came aboard, she wore the dresses and finery her mother had always insisted befitted a "proper" woman. She hated them. It was difficult to maneuver around the ship in the long skirts and petticoats, and her use on board was limited to what she could do in a dress. When they pulled into port in Barbados, Colleen went ashore and found a tailor, commissioning him to make her clothes more suitable for work aboard ship. She also found a cobbler and had him make shoes that would be more comfortable and serviceable than the slippers she wore. In the several days it took to conclude her father's business, the clothes and shoes were finished. She picked up the shoes first, then went to the tailor. She entered the building in a dress and exited in trousers and a tunic, leaving the finery behind. She never wanted it, and she would not don it again if she could help it.

Her duties on board ship were few. She mended the clothes of the men when they needed it and, in self preservation due to the close quarters on board ship, occasionally washed their clothes, as well, when they set ashore and she could get to fresh water. She cut the crewmen's hair when asked and was also a passing fair cook, spending quite a bit of time in the galley. Her mother had indeed schooled her in the things a wife must know, but none of those things truly interested her. She loved the sea and wanted to learn to be a sailor.

When she walked up the gangplank in her new clothes, she went directly to her father, who was plotting a course for their next destination, his mind intent upon this task. He did not look up when Colleen cleared her throat, so she tapped his shoulder and said softly, "Father."

"Can you not see I'm busy, lass? Just give me a few moments." He jotted down several more numbers, then set aside his quill and turned to find his daughter dressed in the garb of a sailor. "What's this?" he said with a laugh as he took in her appearance from her shoes to her hat.

"These are the clothes I intend to wear for my work on the ship, Father. I am of little use in skirts and petticoats, and I wish to learn everything there is to know about the workings of the ship."

"Ah, Colleen, it's not fit work for a woman. And besides, I have told you all I can about—"

"Aye, you have told me. But it's not telling I'm after. I wish to feel the blisters on my hands, the aching in my muscles. I want to know what the view is from the crow's nest and not just from my safe corner on the deck. If the life of a sailor is good enough for you, it's good enough for me, as well. I wish to be a sailor, Father."

Charles knew from the tone of her voice she wasn't going to back down from this. He only hoped in time she would tire of the sea and wish for life on land with a husband and children. But because he could not say no to her, he taught her everything he would have taught his sons.

The years passed as the waves beneath the prow of the ship. She grew to womanhood without spending so much as a fortnight in the awkward stage through which a young girl goes. She grew tall, almost as tall as her father, and her body took on the curves and roundness of a beautiful woman. She knew every inch of the ship like the back of her hand and could climb the riggings like a monkey. Such was her life, and so it remained until July 1717, when Colleen would meet the one person who could make her heart pound within her chest.

Abigail

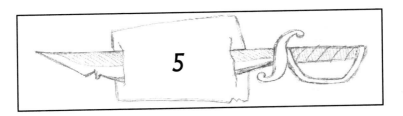

5

Edinburgh, Scotland, 1711

Abigail squirmed as a rivulet of sweat slid between her tightly corseted breasts. The air in Elgin Cathedral seemed so thick she could fairly see it dancing before her eyes, and it was as hot as she could remember. And there she was, bound up in a heavy brocade dress and more petticoats than she had worn in her life, standing beside a man who was naught but a stranger, about to pledge to love and obey him. She turned her eyes toward her mother, seeking a reprieve from this nightmare, but her mother simply gestured for her to turn around and say the vow expected of her to conclude this farce of a wedding. Realizing that only the finish of this blasted ceremony would allow her to change into something more comfortable, with what she hoped did not sound as miserable as she felt, she mumbled, "I will."

With the utterance of those words, Arthur drew her veil over her head as the priest instructed him to kiss the bride. His lips were cold and lifeless, but fortunately, the kiss was quick, so she didn't have to long endure him. She was unable to believe her parents would marry her to this man whom she had met only twice before and had loathed practically on sight. Her mother assured her they were a good match, even though Arthur was twenty-four years her senior and appeared to be a dour and unhappy man.

His family had money, and her family was titled. Arthur's parents were besotted by the notion of their eldest son one day fathering the next earl of Sussex. Not to mention having control over the Hume properties. It was a match that would benefit both families. The feelings of one fourteen-year-old girl mattered little with so much at stake.

The bride and groom exited the church amid a chorus of well wishes and a hailstorm of rice. Arthur's hand rose to protect his face from the white flurry, and he realized his head was bare. He mumbled a soft curse under his breath and tugged on Abby's arm. "I've left my hat in the church. I'll be back in a trice. Wait here." With that, he turned and entered the building. Abby was grateful for any excuse to remove herself from his presence, and she welcomed the arrival of a group of friends who hugged and congratulated her. She could not tell them this was the worst day of her life. She simply smiled grimly and accepted their congratulations without comment.

A loud crack like a clap of thunder rent the air, and the bell in the steeple suddenly lurched to one side, pealing once before dropping through the roof of the church, followed by the timber of the belfry. It sounded as if the entire building might come down, causing all the celebrants but two to make a dash for safety. Only Arthur's father ran toward the church, throwing the doors open wide and calling his son's name as he plunged through a wall of dust and flying debris. Abby stood where Arthur had asked her to wait, unwilling to risk his wrath even at her own peril. He was known as a cruel man by all but her parents, it seemed. She was in no hurry to find out if the stories of his cruelties were true.

The groaning of the old church finally ceased, and several of the men, who had been guests at the wedding, cautiously entered the building to see if help was needed in freeing Arthur from the rubble. Within minutes, Abby heard the sound of a man wailing. Arthur must have been grievously injured to create such a sound, she thought. Thinking that a wife should do what she could to console her husband when he was in pain, she made her way up the steps of the church just as Arthur's father and two other men carried her husband from the wreckage. It was in fact his father keening; from the angle of his head, it would appear that Arthur's neck was broken. Unable to immediately process the enormity of the situation, Abby said, "His hat. He went back for his hat."

Abby stood in the same churchyard three days later. Only instead of a white bridal veil, she wore the black veil of a widow. She planned to continue with the sham of mourning as long as she could, during which time she would be free of the barrage of suitors she had endured up until her parents had settled on Arthur to be her husband. Her mother nudged her arm and nodded toward the grave to indicate she should toss the rose she held onto the casket. She turned away as the blood red flower landed on the wooden box, thinking she should feel some grief for this man who would have been her husband, but instead feeling only that a great weight had been lifted from her shoulders. Her lips involuntarily curved up in a smile as she walked from the grave, her only thought being, *I am free.*

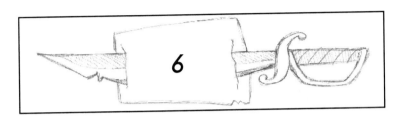

Each year on the anniversary of her husband's death, Abby made a pilgrimage to the churchyard in her black dress and veil. There was no sadness in her heart pushing her to make this homage; grief was not her motivation. As long as she was a widow in mourning, she could not be cajoled into another sham marriage. If wearing black for the rest of her life were the price for independence, she would gladly pay it.

Lord John greeted his wife and daughter as they returned from the fourth such trip to the churchyard, a smile on his handsome face. Abby took after her mother only in shortness of stature, but her strawberry blond hair and sparkling green eyes were the image of her father. "I have some exciting news. A messenger from the king has brought His Majesty's confirmation of my appointment as governor of the Bahamas. And the compensation will allow us to maintain the estate handsomely while we're gone. Not to mention this beastly weather will no longer plague you, my dear."

"The warmth sounds heavenly, John, but can you be sure we'll be safe from the pirates? I understand there has been no appreciable lessening of the marauding in the area. And what of Abby? What are the chances of finding a suitable husband in such a remote part of the world?"

Abby rolled her eyes at her mother's oft-repeated lament about her lack of a husband and the dearth of eligible men within their social class. Shortly after Arthur's death, Abby had spoken to her father and begged for him to allow her to choose her own husband the next time. If she were to marry again, she wished it to be with someone whom she loved. Lord John reluctantly agreed but asked her to at least consider some of the men who had requested her hand since Arthur's death. None met with her approval, and since she still wore the black dress of a widow, the issue was never pressed.

"We shall have a regiment of His Majesty's finest soldiers to protect us, my dear. And there are numerous titled men in the Royal Navy who will call upon our shores. If our Abby cannot find one here who meets with her approval, perhaps a man of the sea can spirit her heart away."

"Och, you should never have left the decision in her hands," Emelia said disdainfully. This was an old argument between the two of them. Emelia simply had to complain about his capitulating to their daughter's wishes at every opportunity. If it had been up to her, Abby would have remarried years before. Emelia's argument was that her own arranged marriage had turned out very well. But in truth, she feared she might not live to see her daughter's children, which pained her more than the rheumatism growing steadily worse with every passing year. Abby was nineteen; had Arthur lived, she could easily have had grandchildren by now who might actually remember their grandmother.

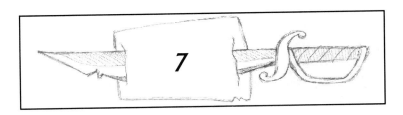

7

"Abigail, come away from there and let the man do his work," Emelia said in a tone of voice that brooked no arguments. Reluctantly, Abby curtsied to the sailor, and with a mumbled apology, walked to where her mother stood clinging to the rigging on the foremast. Since setting sail from Aberdeen almost a fortnight before, Emelia had spent most of the voyage with a slop bucket within reach, and she almost never ventured on deck. When the closeness and the odors below decks finally drove Emelia on deck, she hung on the railings or riggings constantly, her knuckles white from gripping so hard. For her part, Abby was thrilled to be on the open sea, and she knew she probably pestered the sailors far more than she should, but she was eager to know the name for every piece of equipment on board and how it was operated.

"I was not preventing him from working, Mother. I was merely interested in what he was doing. Did you know a coxswain is—"

"I am sure I have never heard of a coxswain, nor do I wish to. But if you feel you absolutely must study the workings of the ship, why not seek out the bonny captain and learn from him?"

"Aye, he's bonny, but he can't hold an intelligent conversation upon any subject beyond himself. Bartholomew told me his rank was bought and paid for by his rich father. A barnacle would make a more entertaining companion than the captain, I think."

"Perhaps, but he is rich and a fine-looking fellow. You could do worse."

"Mother, I can also do better." Emelia opened her mouth to say something, but Abby went on hurriedly before she could interrupt. "And I know you and Father made a fine match without ever having laid eyes upon each other beforehand, but do you ken, yours is a rare pairing indeed. I wish to love my husband, not merely tolerate him. It is my life, after all."

"That it is. But I tell you truly, if you don't lower your expectations somewhat, you may find yourself alone and unprotected when you're older. I can't help but worry. You're my only daughter. I want what's best for you, you know that."

"Aye, I do." She linked her arm through her mother's and kissed her lightly on the cheek. "Now if only we could agree on what 'best' is." Abby had to laugh at the little pout upon her mother's face at the utterance of those words. Placing her fingers to the sides of Emelia's lips, Abby pushed up until the frown had become a somewhat lopsided grin. Shaking her head at her daughter's antics, Emelia joined in the laughter.

Abby dozed in a loosely rigged hammock on the forecastle, the skirt of the dress she had been mending pooled on the deck around her. The sound of many feet pounding the deck roused her, and she jerked, poking herself sharply in her finger with the needle she still held. Martin, a boatswain whom she had befriended, came running up to her with a smile on his face.

"Beg pardon, Miss Hume, but I thought you might want to be up and about to get your first look at Nassau, your new home."

"Oh, yes. Thank you, Martin." Abby let the dress fall to the deck and raced after Martin to the bow of the ship. The island that glittered in the tropical sun looked very much like others where their ship had stopped for supplies during the two-month journey from England. But this was to be home; she thought the water a bit greener than around those other islands. And the sky was blue beyond belief. She knew already she would have to buy some new paints if she hoped to capture these brilliant hues. There was also a rather large house, just visible over the tops of the trees. Since it appeared to be the largest in sight, she surmised it was the governor's mansion. She turned at the touch of a hand on her shoulder to find her father looking down with a huge smile on his face. Abby wrapped her arms around his waist and pointed at the house barely visible through the trees. "Is that our house, Father?"

His gaze followed her finger. "I expect it is, my sweet. What a beautiful view of the harbor we shall have from up there, eh?"

"Indeed, it seems the entire island will be visible. And the sky is so clear, I would not be surprised if we could see all the way back to Scotland from there. I will need more paints and canvas than I brought, Father. I plan to spend most of my time with a paintbrush in my hand. Unless you have other duties for me, of course." Her enthusiasm infected Lord Hume, and he took her into his arms and whirled her around, something he had not done since she was a child.

"You will need to participate in social functions, my dear. Even here in this outpost, I suspect we will be entertaining a fair amount of people. And of course, you must attend your mother and learn all the tasks expected of a proper British lady. Remember, it is the king of England who sent us here."

Abby knew what her father truly meant was she would be expected to take her mother's place when she was abed with one of her all-too-numerous headaches. "I'm not British, Father, I'm Scots. And we Scots know all those tasks from birth."

Lord Hume laughed and kissed her on the forehead. "What is the source of all this merriment?" Lady Emelia came up behind them just as they burst into laughter. The sound was infectious, and she was soon laughing along with them. The trio stood with their arms locked around one another as they watched their future approaching.

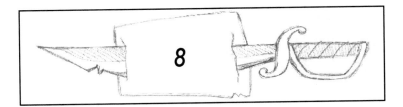

8

The *Betsy Ann* pulled into Nassau harbor on a bright July morning. Their cargo was spices and tea from the Indies, and they were to take on a cargo of rum for the return trip. They also had papers from the Crown to be delivered to the governor, and this task was given to Colleen.

The governor's mansion was the most opulent building on the island, and her steps slowed as she approached to allow her to take in the beauty of the building. Instead of going directly to the door, she walked around the house to the seaward side, knowing the view from there would be spectacular.

There was a verandah behind the house, and on it a young woman sat with an easel before her. She patiently applied daubs of color from a palette she held in her hand to the canvas on the easel. The painting was of the sea and the surrounding hills and vegetation. Colleen approached on cat feet, loath to disturb the woman at her work, but wishing to get a closer look. She stopped several feet away and simply stared; the painting was beautiful but even more beautiful was the lady herself. Her hair was as bright as the morning sun, and it cascaded over her shoulders in curls. Colleen could only see her in profile, but she could tell by the curve of her lips and the tilt of her nose the face would be a vision. She took a few steps closer, and just as she did, the painter turned her head toward the tree she was painting, and Colleen froze in her tracks.

"You might as well stop skulking in the bushes. I see you," the lady said playfully.

"I ... I was not skulking, I was admiring your work. And I'm not in the bushes, but in plain sight on the verandah."

The voice surprised the painter; she had thought it was a man from the glimpse she had of the clothes. She put her palette down and turned in her seat to get a better look at her unannounced visitor. Her breath caught in her throat at the woman standing before her. She was garbed as a sailor, but there the resemblance to a man ended. Her long black hair framed a face as magnificent as any she had ever seen. The eyes made the blue of the ocean seem dull by comparison, and her full lips were coral-colored and shaped at the moment like the letter O. She gathered her wits about her at last and smiled at her visitor.

"Come closer then and get a better look. I'll not bite you."

For her part, Colleen was smitten from the first look into the painter's impish face. She was not sure her legs would hold her and more certain they would not be able to carry her closer to the vision in the peach-colored dress. She willed herself to move, and at last her feet began a hesitant shuffle that brought her within a few feet of the painter. She looked away from the woman and at the painting because it was expected of her. But her choice would have been to do nothing for the rest of her life but stare into the lovely face looking up at her from the chair.

"Well, what do you think then?"

"I ... it ... I ... you mean the painting? It is ... masterful. I have never seen such work, truly. You are gifted." And she meant every word. For she had not looked upon a painting more true to the subject it depicted, and yet at the same time, showing so much more than what was there. A bit of the painter herself was on the canvas, she was certain.

"Och, you are a flatterer. But thank you, kind lady. 'Tis rude of me not to introduce myself. I am Abigail Hume. My father is Lord John Hume, governor of this territory." Colleen bowed in acknowledgment of the status of the beautiful painter.

"I am Colleen Edwards, daughter of Charles Edwards Esquire, Captain of the *Betsy Ann*, hailing from Hartlepool, my lady."

Abby laughed, the sound musical to Colleen's ears. "I am not the lady of this house, Miss Edwards. My mother holds that title. I am simply..."

Breathtaking, Colleen finished in her head.

"...a would-be painter and not really a very good one for all that," Abby said with another laugh.

"I beg to differ, Miss Hume. I think you are an exceedingly good painter. I would think anyone would be honored to hang one of your paintings on their wall."

"Then you shall have one to hang on your wall, as I have a cabinet full of them, but only if you will call me Abby."

Colleen could scarcely believe she would actually give her one of her paintings, but she was not going to argue. "'Tis little enough payment for one of your fine paintings, Abby. But you must also call me Colleen, or Col if you prefer, which is what my father calls me."

"The bargain is struck then, Colleen. Come with me into the house, and you may pick whichever one strikes your fancy. I would give you this one, but it is not quite finished, and the paint will be a long time drying." Abby covered her palette with a cloth soaked with turpentine to keep the paint from drying and pushed it under her chair out of the sun.

Colleen's heart pounded as she followed Abby into the cool interior of the house.

It was approaching Christmas when next the *Betsy Ann* called at the port of Nassau. Colleen could scarcely contain her excitement at the prospect of once again seeing the governor's lovely daughter, who was never out of her mind for more than a few moments at a time. She marveled that she was able to complete her tasks aboard ship without inflicting harm upon herself, so given was she to daydreaming about Abby. And of course, the painting with her dainty signature on it was suspended beside her bunk on board the *Betsy Ann*, where it was the last thing she saw at night and the first thing she saw in the morning. All Colleen knew of Abby, other than the fact that she was the most beautiful creature she had ever seen, was that she was a painter. With Christmas approaching, Colleen was ever on the alert for something she might purchase for Abby to use for her painting. In a shop in South Carolina, she found a lovely wooden box containing three paint brushes of different sizes and textures she thought would be perfect. This very box was wrapped in the finest paper she could find in the colonies and rested snugly inside her pocket. She could not wait to see Abby's face as she opened the gift.

Colleen paced the deck, impatient for the man on the dock to secure the gangplank so she could leave the ship, which at that moment felt like tar holding her in place. Just as she was about to make a rude comment to the man on the dock, he signaled with a wave to let her know she could safely disembark. "About bloody well time," she muttered under her breath. The moment she stepped off the gangplank, she lit out for the governor's mansion as if her feet had taken wing. Taking just a few minutes at the crest of the hill to catch her breath, she flew around the side of the house, hoping to find the object of many of her dreams, both waking and sleeping, at work on another painting. But such was not the case that day.

Abby was in the parlor practicing her piano lessons, which was, according to her mother, another of the skills a fine lady must possess, but her heart was not in her playing. On a good day Abby was able to divert her thoughts from the beautiful Colleen for long enough to turn out a passable melody or two, but it had been months since they had been together, and she was missing Colleen to the point of distraction.

Abby sighed and took her hands from the keyboard and looked out the window—just in time to see the one who haunted her dreams walking away. Rising from her stool, she fairly flew to the front door. Throwing it wide open, she called, "Colleen!"

Colleen was making her way down the long carriage drive when she heard her name. Turning, she saw Abby standing in the doorway, gesturing with her hand for her to come back. A smile lit up Colleen's face and she ran back up to the house. Abby was standing there, smiling and shaking her head, hands on hips.

"Why did you not knock on the door then, Col? Were you just going to walk away without so much as a how do you do?"

Colleen blushed and lowered her eyes. Now that she was actually here again, she realized she had no real reason for her visit, and she could not think of a thing to say besides, "How do you do, Abby?"

"Very well since you're here. Mother is having one of her sick headaches, and Father is off being governor. I was just about to have a bit of supper all alone, and you can relieve me of the boredom of my own company if you would kindly agree to join me."

"It would be my pure pleasure if it's not too much trouble."

"Not a bit of trouble. Cook was just about to ... oh, I've an idea. Let's have Cook pack us a basket with some cold chicken and bread and cheese. We can go have a bit of a picnic by the water. I've been trapped in this house by the rain for days and am about to go mad for some fresh air."

The idea of being alone with Abby away from the house both terrified and pleased Colleen, who responded immediately. "It would be wonderful to share a meal with one so lovely as you."

"You flatter me. It is I who will have the pleasure of seeing your beautiful face across from me. Please, come and sit in the parlor while I make the arrangements." Once again Colleen followed her into her magnificent home. She perched on the edge of a chair in the parlor, not daring to lean against the cloth back of the chair in a tunic more than clean enough for the ship but questionable in such a spotless home. It seemed hours she sat there, but it could only have been minutes before Abby returned with a large picnic basket.

"Here, let me take that heavy basket," Colleen said, extending her hand. Abby obediently handed it to her, and Colleen grunted at the weight. "Good God, have you put the entire kitchen in here?"

Abby laughed, then put her finger to her lips and said in a conspiratorial tone, "No, but I have managed to sneak a bottle of Father's favorite Jamaican rum in there. We shall dine and drink in style."

"If I do not collapse from carrying this to the beach," Colleen grumbled good-naturedly.

"Oh, you are a fine strong lass. I suspect you could carry much heavier than this tiny basket," Abby teased. "Come on, let's get out of here before Mother recovers and sends me back to my piano playing."

Not needing a second warning, Colleen hefted the basket and with a bow she said, "After you, my lady."

"Oh, I shall never eat another bite again," Colleen groaned. It seemed as if Abby had brought nearly enough food to feed the entire crew of the *Betsy Ann*, and the two of them had consumed it all. The bottle of rum was almost empty, as well, and Colleen's head was pleasantly filled with warm thoughts of her companion, who was similarly sated and light-headed.

The two women lay side by side on the blanket Abby had fetched as they were leaving the house. The rum bottle was between them, an easy reach for either one. Abby was lying on her back, her eyes closed, absorbing the warmth of the sun on her skin. "This feels glorious," she said softly. "I could fall asleep and stay here forever."

"Ah, but you would not be able to paint while lying upon your back...."

"I'm sure I could. Michelangelo painted the entire ceiling of the Sistine Chapel while lying on his back. A Scots woman is capable of many things, why—"

Colleen laughed. "I don't doubt your skills for a moment, dear lady. I suspect you could paint the sky itself if you wanted to. And I hope this humble gift will help should you decide to do just that." She drew the package from her pocket and placed it in Abby's hand. The look of surprise on her face was worth traipsing through all of the shops Colleen visited in her quest to find the perfect gift. "Merry Christmas, Abby. I know it's a bit early, but I'm not at all certain where we will be when the twenty-fifth arrives, and I wanted you to have this."

"Colleen—dear sweet lass—what have I done to deserve such a precious friend as you?"

Colleen rolled the word "friend" around in her mind and knew it was inadequate to describe her feelings for Abby. Friendship certainly was part of what she felt, but something much deeper clutched at her stomach when she thought of Abby, and her heart ached when they were apart. That was certainly not the way friends thought of each other, at least not in her experience. She glanced up to see Abby looking at her strangely and realized she was waiting for a response, or perhaps thinking Colleen had not heard her. "I'm not sure how to answer that. I only know I want to give you things that will please you. And it's you who are precious, beyond measure. You gave me a beautiful painting when we were practically strangers. I wanted to give something to you in return. Now open it, please."

Without further encouragement, Abby sat up on the blanket and began to carefully remove the string from the package. Colleen laughed and reached into her boot to remove the knife she carried there. "Let me cut the string, Abby. It will take forever to—"

"No, Col. I want to remove it all in one piece. How impatient you are." She dropped the string onto the blanket and proceeded to unfold the paper, taking her time with that task, as well. When Colleen began to laugh again, Abby punched her lightly in the arm. "Apparently you English girls are not schooled in the art of neatness," she said. "I wish to keep this paper…" Her voice trailed off as she opened the wooden box to reveal the fine quality brushes inside. "Oh, Colleen, these are the most beautiful brushes I've ever seen. Thank you so much!" She set the box aside and threw herself into Colleen's arms.

Colleen was caught off-guard and tumbled backward, and of course Abby followed, since her arms were firmly around Colleen's waist. Unable to think what to say while staring into Abby's sea green eyes, Colleen said, "There's a horsehair one and another made from … rabbit, I think. Or some other creature…"

"Hush," Abby whispered, her lips so close to Colleen's, the tiny exhalation caressed her skin. With a groan, Colleen closed her eyes. Before Abby could truly think about what she was doing, she brushed her lips over Colleen's, surprised to find them so soft. She pulled back, watching as Colleen opened her eyes, an unreadable look reflected in their depths. "I'm sorry if I…" Abby started, but Colleen stopped her with a finger to her lips.

"No, never be sorry for what you feel, Abby. I treasure your honesty as much as I treasure your heart." She found she was unable to divert her gaze from the adorable face above her. While memorizing every freckle and dimple, Colleen could not fail to notice the alarming shade of pink that had spread across Abby's cheeks and nose.

"I'm afraid you're burning rather badly. Perhaps we should get you out of the sun."

Abby rolled on her side and opened her eyes to look into

Colleen's face. "Must we?"

Colleen nodded; she would be content to stay here, but she truly feared for Abby's health if they remained where they were.

"There is a cave just down the beach. The sun will not reach me there. Do you need to be back on your ship soon?"

"Not until sundown. Come, let's get you under some shelter." She stood up and extended her hand to Abby, who grasped it firmly. She tugged Abby to her feet but was in no hurry to release her hand. Apparently, Abby was content, as well, because she made no move to take her hand away. Colleen retrieved the bottle of rum and the blanket, but left the basket to be collected on their way back. Wordlessly, Abby led the way to the cave.

"It's underwater during high tide and hard to find from the sea or the house. I found the place during one of my many long walks. I've spent hours sitting at the mouth of the cave, painting the beach and the rocks."

"I know. I have that painting on my wall. It makes me think of you—every day." They spread the blanket just inside the cave out of reach of the fierce tropical sun. Colleen leaned against the cave wall, and Abby rested on the blanket with her head on Colleen's thigh. Neither woman seemed particularly bothered by the physical closeness. Since the moment Colleen took Abby's hand and lifted her from the beach, they had been in constant contact. It felt—right.

"Have you ... do you ever think you might give up the sea one day? Perhaps get married and have children?"

"Give up the sea? It seems unlikely. I am at home there, as I have never been on land. I might be persuaded to plant myself on land if the right person asked me." She looked down at Abby, the thought running through her mind ... *you have but to ask, and I would be wherever you wanted me to be*. Abby said nothing, keeping her own counsel. With a sigh, Colleen continued. "But marry ... no. I have no desire to be a brood mare to some stallion who desires my father's wealth. I would as soon go down with the ship."

"My father has all but given up on getting me to marry again."

"Again? You were married before?"

"I was married when I was fourteen. It was an arranged marriage. My husband was killed on our wedding day. I wish I could say I'm not glad he died, but truly, I would rather have been in prison than harnessed to that man for life. Since then, my father has brought many young men to my door, but I've not found one whom I could envision myself spending a lifetime with. I will only marry for love." Abby's sea green eyes looked up into the blue ones above her. "And the love I have found, I can't marry." Tears leaked from her eyes to stain Colleen's trousers.

"And is marriage so important then?" Colleen softly asked. "Is the love itself not enough?" She wiped the tears from Abby's cheeks.

"I wish ... I wish it could be so. But my father ... I'm afraid he would disown me, shun me. I don't know if I could live with his scorn."

"If I were a bard, I would write sonnets describing the musical sound of your laughter, the depths of the light in your eyes, your lips that beg to be kissed. And every sonnet would proclaim my undying love for you. If I were a minstrel, I would set those sonnets to music, rhapsodies so sweet the angels would weep to hear them. Or ... if I had your skills with the paintbrush, I would spend all my waking hours trying to capture your beauty on canvas. But there are not enough hours in the day, nor would my skill be great enough to truly do you justice." She brushed one finger lightly over Abby's lips and felt the exhalation of breath as she sighed.

"I dared not hope you might feel the same way I do," Abby said softly. "In truth, I think I loved you from the first moment you spoke to me." Abby sat up on the floor of the cave, then turned so she was facing Colleen, their lips only a breath apart. She raised her hand to touch Colleen's hair, then twined her fingers in the silky dark tresses. Surely, she had never touched anything quite so soft in her life, and the thought that soon Colleen would be once again out of her reach made her sigh. "If my lips beg to be kissed, it would only be your kiss they yearn for." She leaned in until their lips met, soft on soft, at first the chaste kiss of friends. Then

Colleen's lips parted, and her tongue began a timid exploration of Abby's lips, begging for entrance. Abby granted it without hesitation. Growing bolder, Colleen twined her fingers in the golden curls of Abby's head and pulled her up against her body. At the first touch of Abby's breasts against her own, Colleen could not suppress the trembles that raced up and down her body. Abby moaned softly, the sound a whisper against Colleen's mouth.

"I can't tell you how many times I've wished to be close to you like this," Colleen said as they broke apart to gasp for breath. Their hearts pounded so loudly, Colleen was certain the sound was as loud outside the cave as the drums of the natives of the island. Abby snuggled against Colleen's chest, her eyes closed in contentment. "I wish we could stay here forever, but the tide is coming in and we must get out of this cave while we still can."

Abby opened her eyes and saw that indeed the water was almost touching the blanket upon which they lay. She jumped to her feet, extending her hand to Colleen and helping her up. Colleen grasped the blanket and wrapped it in a bundle, quickly handing it to Abby and scooping her up in her arms.

Colleen was about to dash into the now ankle-high water when Abby stiffened in her arms. "Wait ... the rum," Abby said, laughing. Perhaps they could find another spot out of the sun to pass some time before Colleen must return to her ship, and the rum was a great reducer of inhibitions. Colleen lowered her to bring the neck of the bottle within Abby's grasp, and once it was secured, she made a dash for higher ground.

Unfortunately, there was to be no further drinking or kissing this day. Even as they made their way up the beach, one of Abby's father's servants was standing on the bluff, calling her name. "Coming!" she called in response, her face a mask of disappointment.

"Perhaps tomorrow we can manage to steal some time for each other. My father does not plan to sail until two days hence."

Abby shook her head. "My mother has asked me to accompany her tomorrow to tea with a flock of her stuffy friends. I don't think I can beg off at this late hour."

Now it was Colleen's face that revealed her unhappiness at

having to leave the island without further contact with the woman she loved. "I'll come to call when my father's business brings us once again to your shores. I hope you'll not give your heart to another while I'm gone." Her tone was playful, but at the same time she knew it was not unusual for girls to be married off by their parents with little more than a by-your-leave, and should such a fate once again befall Abby, Colleen saw no reason to continue living.

"How could I give it to another when it is traveling all over the world with you, bonny lass?" The servant who had called her was now making his way over the dunes toward them and would soon be within earshot. "Perhaps you should leave from the beach instead of the house. I'm not sure I want the servants letting my father know I was on the beach with a sailor. God knows what he might think."

"Until the next time then ..." She kissed Abby briefly on the lips, then turned and ran up the beach toward town.

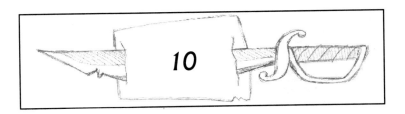

10

"Abby, come inside! You'll catch your death out in this downpour!" Emelia stood in the verandah doorway, waving to try to catch her daughter's attention. But Abby's eyes were looking toward the port, where she caught sight of a familiar vessel at the dock. Her desire was so great to not miss Colleen if she should call, Abby requested to have several trees removed from her sightline to the dock. She told her mother she wished to paint the dock, and the trees were an impediment, but the reality was Colleen had called one time when Abby was out, and they were not able to get together that trip. Most schooners looked about the same from a distance, so the next time the *Betsy Ann* called at Nassau, Abby gave Colleen a bright blue scarf that very nearly matched her eyes and asked her to fly it from the rigging when they pulled into port so she would know not to leave the house before Colleen could get there. Normally, she would wait on the verandah, pretending to paint, and if Colleen did not have a message to deliver for the governor to justify calling at the house, she would approach from the beach and whistle a sea chantey to let Abby know she was there.

"Miss Hume, Her Ladyship asked me to come fetch you into the house." The sound of the servant's voice made Abby jump as she had not seen him approach. He opened an umbrella above her head and stood patiently waiting for her to comply with her mother's request. With a sigh, Abby turned and walked toward the house, the servant dutifully following behind with the umbrella held aloft. She knew there was no point in continuing to ignore her mother; Emelia was relentless and would send every servant in the house if need be to bring her wayward daughter inside.

Emelia waited by the door with a thick cape. Clucking, she draped it over Abby's shoulders the moment she came in. "Abigail, what can you be thinking standing out there in the rain until you are soaked to the skin? And please don't tell me you were planning to paint in this deluge."

"No, Mother, I was watching the ships come in. It … soothes me to think that even in the midst of such a storm, the vessels are able to find their way to safety." The rain had been pounding the island for the better part of two days, and in truth, Abby had been worried that Colleen might be out there in the thick of it. Colleen had told her she hoped to have returned to Nassau several days earlier, and Abby's fear mounted with each passing hour. Until she saw the blue scarf whipping in the wind and rain.

"Well, there is nothing you can do for the ships at sea, so it seems pointless to continue to scour the port. Unless…" Her mother's voice shifted from the clucking hen to the hopeful future grandmother. "…there might be someone out there who has caught your fancy. Captain Thompson is a fine figure of a man, with a home not so very far from Edinburgh. Why you could—"

Abby rolled her eyes and said in a petulant tone of voice, "Oh, please, Mother. I've told you, Captain Thompson bores me beyond belief. You have endured those insufferable teas with him as well as I. Surely, you know how I feel about him. If I never see his 'fine figure' again, I will be truly happy."

The man could speak of nothing but himself—his prowess as a swordsman, his rank in the Royal Navy, as well as the fine ancestral home he had inherited from his father. And from his interactions with the servants and other lower class citizens of Nassau, it was clear he differed from Arthur only in that he was handsome. She had no reason to think his indifference to a wife should differ greatly from the disdain he showed to her. Nothing could force her to endure another social event with the captain if she could help it.

Emelia planted her hands on her hips and leveled a stern gaze at Abby. "If not him, then what man is it who draws your attention toward the port on such a God-awful day as this? You can't fool me, Abby. I know there's someone. You can talk to me."

"No, Mother, no man has captured my heart, and I wish you would simply let the matter rest. If you wish for me to talk with you, please, I beg you, drop this line of inquiry." Abby turned and started toward the stairs but was stopped by the pleading sound of her mother's voice.

"Abby, it's only because I love you that I wish for you to find some happiness. You seem so sad most of the time. I simply can't bear it. Surely you know this to be true."

"I do, Mother, truly." Abby wrapped her arms around Emelia's neck and gave her a kiss on the cheek. "And I love you so much for caring. I promise you, when I am able to finally give my heart and receive your blessing, you will be the first person I'll come to. But until then, please let it be. If you'll excuse me, I'm going to go get into some dry clothes. I'll be down for tea."

"All right, dear. I believe I'll retire to my rooms. I feel a headache coming on." Abby saw the telltale signs of an impending headache in the way her mother squinted her eyes and felt a twinge of guilt that perhaps their conversation had brought on the pain.

"Oh, I'm sorry. Would you like me to fetch you a glass of water and your headache powders?"

"No need. I have them by my bed. I'll join you for tea if I'm feeling up to it." Emelia kissed Abby's cheek lightly and patted her hand before making her way slowly up the stairs.

Abby started to follow but decided to make a stop at the kitchen first to get a pitcher of warm water to freshen up with after changing her clothes. Before she could reach her destination, however, she was intercepted by a servant bearing a tray upon which she could see a calling card.

"Beg pardon, Miss Hume, but there is a gentleman caller who says he has a message that can be delivered only to yourself."

He extended the tray so she could take up the card, and a smile curved her lips as she read the name "Charles Edwards, Esquire." She assumed Colleen had sent an emissary in her stead, but the name of her father on the card gave no question as to whom the true sender might be.

"Thank you, Joshua. Will you please show him into the parlor and tell him I will join him there directly?" With that, she virtually flew up the stairs, so intent was she to don some fresh clothing and find out what news there was of Colleen.

It seemed her chambermaid had grown extra thumbs since morning when she had assisted her at dressing, so inept was she at even the simplest of tasks. Susan was very nearly in tears from being remonstrated so often for her clumsiness, when Abby finally realized the girl's discomfort. Taking a deep breath, she smiled and said, "I'm sorry for my shortness with you, Susan. There's a guest waiting for me, and I'm loath to keep him waiting any longer than necessary. I will try to stand still and make your job somewhat easier." And having said so, she did just that, and within a few minutes, she was dressed and ready to go, her hair still a bit damp from her time outside, but there was nothing to be done for it.

Abby stood up as tall as she could, which given her diminutive stature meant not very tall at all. She drew her shoulders back and raised her chin, intent upon representing herself as well as she could for Colleen's shipmate, for she assumed her caller to be none other. Opening the parlor door, her first sight was of the tall form of a well-dressed sailor; indeed, he appeared to be an officer, uncharacteristically still wearing his three-cornered hat indoors. His back was to her as he warmed himself in front of the fire.

"Sir, I am Miss Abigail Hume. I believe you have a message for me from Charles Edwards of the *Betsy Ann*."

"Nay, not from Charles, my lady." The voice was familiar, yet deeper than what she would have expected. Nevertheless, when her caller turned away from the fireplace, Abby beheld the piercing blue eyes and beautiful smile belonging to Colleen herself. It appeared as if her breasts had been bound, for the voluptuous woman she knew her to be had apparently been replaced by a very handsome man.

Closing the door behind her, Abby flew the several feet required to reach Colleen. She very nearly threw herself into Colleen's arms but halted a few steps away when she realized that at any moment a servant could enter the room, and it would not do to be found in a compromising position with a man.

"I apologize for the ruse, Abby, but I could not have borne it if I'd made this trek only to find you gone again. And I thought perhaps your family would look more favorably upon a gentleman caller than a woman, particularly if he were the son of a captain of one of His Majesty's privateers." And saying this, she bowed low, removing her three-cornered hat and allowing her black tresses to tumble about her shoulders.

"Oh, Colleen, you cannot imagine my mother's happiness if I were to receive a gentleman caller whom I did not detest almost upon sight." She reached up to caress the free-flowing curls of the woman she had to admit she loved more than she believed possible to love a man. "But if she came into this room now, I fear she would faint dead away. Much as I hate to have you do it, will you please once again tuck your hair up under your hat? I'm sure I could more easily explain a man with his hat on inside the house than a woman dressed as a man."

"I understand. This is why I had not removed the hat, but I know your fondness for running your fingers through the length of my hair and thought you might want to do so just once before I don the hat again." She twisted her hair into something of a knot and held it on her head with one hand while putting on the hat with the other. "Is that better, my lady?"

"Better? No, for I would prefer it if your hair framed your beautiful face as it did the first time I saw you on the verandah. But for the sake of appearances, it is better to maintain the ruse. And by the way, you do make a most handsome fellow." She stepped to a sideboard where a decanter of brandy and glasses sat upon a tray and poured a small amount into two glasses. When she turned around again and beheld the most beautiful person she had ever seen, her breath caught in her throat, and she had to take a moment to compose herself. At last, with a smile, she handed one glass to Colleen, and in a mock salute to her beloved, she raised her own glass to her lips. Colleen followed suit, draining nearly all of the fine brandy in one swallow. Abby wanted so badly to reach out and touch the lips still slightly moist from the liquor but stopped herself short of doing so. With a sigh, she said, "I've no doubt my mother would have no objection should I announce to her my intention to marry someone like you."

Colleen laughed, "Someone like me? Surely there is no one quite as mad as I am, to have borrowed my father's finest uniform only to dash through a downpour for the chance of spending a few minutes in your presence. I can't imagine how I'm going to explain its condition to him."

"No, not someone like you, only you." A thought came into her head, and she said with a smile, "How many days will you be in port here?"

"We leave with the tide day after tomorrow. Have you something in mind?"

"I'm scheduled to spend the morning tomorrow at my piano lesson and later in the day to have tea with some of the girls. I can send a message to the piano teacher to tell her I'm not well and to tell the girls I will not be at tea. I'll then have nearly the entire day to spend with you. Are you able to get free from your duties on board ship for a while?"

"To be with you? Absolutely. As long as you are certain you can carry out your scheme without bringing trouble upon yourself."

"Bah, I would deal with any trouble we might face, as long as we can spend time together. And I believe I know just the place."

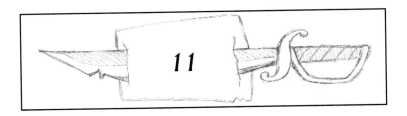

Colleen and Abby arranged to meet at the governor's boathouse, which was far enough from the house to avoid detection. And since her father was away, the boathouse was empty, so they could remain there as long as they liked. It was more than just a boathouse; apparently, the builder thought the governor might require a small place to get away from his ... duties. It was outfitted with a small parlor with a couch almost large enough to serve as a bed. Abby was sure her mother was not aware of this extra room, or she might be watching her husband a bit closer when he was supposed to be out on the business of governing the islands. But Abby knew, even if her mother did not, that her father was completely devoted to his wife. And thus she also knew the little parlor had never been used by anyone, except for the occasional drink of brandy her father took to warm himself before making the trek up to the house.

The morning dawned bright and clear, the only reminders of the previous day's storm the debris littering the beach as far as the eye could see. Abby sent Joshua on an errand to her music teacher early in the morning, and shortly after he returned to say her message had been delivered, she set out with a sheaf of music under her arm, brushing off her mother's suggestion she take

Susan with her as she normally did.

"Mother, I am twenty years old, certainly old enough to walk the short distance from here to Miss Harwood's home and back. Besides, Susan has enough work to do here to keep her busy for most of the day." Abby had pulled the hem on two of her dresses and begged Susan to hem them straight away so she might wear them. With a smile on her face she could not seem to remove, Abby set off down the path toward town, and as soon as she was no longer in sight of the house, she turned off across the dunes and backtracked to the little house on the water. She was grateful her father had shown her where he kept the spare key to the place in case of emergency, and she pulled it out of her bag, where she'd also put some bread, cheese, and fruit for later. Opening the door, she set about drawing up the sashes and dusting off the table before placing the food upon it. The room was somewhat musty from disuse, but she hoped to have it smelling fresh by the time Colleen arrived. She struck a flint to the whale oil lamp that was the only source of light in the room, and as it caught, the shadows fled into the corners.

A freshwater stream ran very near to the boathouse, and Colleen stopped there to fill a vase she had brought with her from the ship. Into this, she placed the small bouquet of flowers she'd gathered on her way. As she drew near to the boathouse, she could hear the sounds of singing from within. The melody was familiar but slightly different than what she was used to hearing on the docks. But there was no doubt it was Jean Adam's song "The Mariner's Wife," for the lyrics were the same. Colleen was careful to avoid making noise as she approached the little house; she didn't want to startle Abby and cause her to stop singing. Colleen was singing along in her head until Abby reached the line, which should have said, "Is this a time to think o' work? When Colin's at the door?" She felt a tightening about her heart when Abby sang instead, "When Colleen's at the door."

"Aye, that she is," Colleen said softly when Abby had finished the song, causing Abby to jump.

"You'll be the death of me if you continue to creep up as

you do, Colleen Edwards." The smile on her face at the sight of the woman she loved did not match the words she spoke, but nonetheless Colleen held out the vase of flowers as if it were a peace offering before she stepped into the room.

"I didn't want to disturb your singing, so I tried to be as quiet as I could. Forgive me if I frightened you. And I have to say, I'm awed by your talents as a singer, which rival your painting skills for tugging at the heart strings. It surprised me also to learn you even knew such a song."

Abby took the vase of flowers and placed it on the table, cocking her head once or twice to make sure it was centered just so. When she turned around, Colleen was directly behind her, hands behind her back and a grin on her face. "Do not think you can flatter me into not being angry with you for scaring me out of a year's growth. Which, given my stature, I can ill afford to lose." Colleen chuckled, and Abby slapped her lightly on the arm. "And I learned the song from my chambermaid when we lived in Edinburgh. A superstitious creature, she was, and always sang that song when her husband was out to sea. Thought it would bring him home safely."

"And did it? Bring him home safely, I mean?"

"Oh, aye. He gave up the sea to become a farmer. But while replacing some thatch on his roof, he slid off and broke his neck. He was safer at sea."

Colleen could not stifle an involuntary laugh, and she lowered her eyes so the smile lingering on her face could not be seen. "My apologies. I did not mean to appear insensitive to your chambermaid's tragic plight."

Abby tried to maintain her decorum, but Colleen's smile was contagious, and she laughed in spite of herself. "It was horrible, truly. Poor dear never smiled again after that, and she'd always been so gay and lively before. I found myself almost wishing I could shake her back into her old self. But never mind, she is thousands of miles from here. And why are we talking about her when we have so little time together?"

"I'm sure I don't know, and for my part, the subject is closed. Perhaps we could start over." She pulled a bundle from behind her back and held it out to Abby, whose face lit up as if Christmas had come again. Seeing the look on Abby's face, Colleen nearly withdrew the package. "It isn't so much, really. Just a small token..."

Abby snatched the package from her hands and proceeded to untie the string that held it closed. "It doesn't matter what it is. The fact you thought of me while you ... oh!" With paper and string discarded, Abby beheld the most elegant-looking handkerchief she'd ever seen. It was cream-colored linen with a lace border in a matching color. In the corner, the initials *AH* were embroidered in a neat stitch with a green thread that was a near match for Abby's eyes. "Oh, Colleen, this is beautiful. Wherever did you find such fine linen? I have never seen the like of it."

"It's from the factory of Samuel-Louis Crommelin in Lisburn. He is the overseer of the royal linen manufactured in Ireland."

"And who has done such a delicate job of tatting the lace and applying the embroidering?"

Embarrassed by all the compliments, Colleen's cheeks flushed red. "I'm flattered to hear you appreciate the work. I did it myself, but I'm nowhere near as skilled as my mother, who taught me all I know."

"My mother taught me all I know, as well, and I could not do such a job as this to save my life. Your mother is to be commended for her skills both as a teacher and with the needle."

"I wish she were alive to hear your words. I always felt somewhat inadequate when I was learning, despite her reassurances. It's been a long time since I've attempted to make something like this. I'm glad it was not a total muddle."

While Colleen spoke, Abby laid out the simple meal she brought, placing the handkerchief Colleen gave her by her plate to use as a napkin. When she was finished, she gestured for Colleen to sit and took the seat opposite her at the small table.

"I wish I could have known her. Please, paint me a picture of her with words so that I may see her."

Colleen picked up a piece of pineapple from the plate in front of her and brought it to her lips. When the juice ran down her chin, Abby quickly wiped the mess away with the handkerchief Colleen made for her. She smiled at Abby; where to begin to describe her precious mother? At last, she drew a breath and began. "In appearance, she was a typical English woman—very fair of skin, with a sprinkling of freckles dotting her face, particularly in the summer when she worked in the garden. Her eyes were green, very like yours, as I remember. And she had laugh lines that crinkled when she smiled and dimples that gave her face an impish look. Her height was not so great, but she was taller than you."

"That's not saying much. Everybody is taller than me," Abby said.

Colleen laughed. "Nay, not so. I saw a woman in India who would not have reached your waist. Of course, she had no legs—"

"Oh, stop," Abby said playfully, batting Colleen on the arm again. "Now finish telling me about your mother. I can almost see her, and she's beautiful like her daughter."

"Her beauty was in her smile and in the way her eyes danced with merriment. She had a lovely singing voice and frequently would burst into song as she went about her chores. One could not help but smile to hear her. And she was the most caring of mothers, none of us lacked for anything. She was also fiercely independent, with a most stubborn streak. Her own parents died when she was young, and she was raised in an orphanage staffed by nuns. It was they who taught her to sew and embroider, and she was soon doing much finer work than the nuns themselves. They took to sending her to the market to sell her wares and word spread about her work. She met my father while delivering some linen to the home of my Aunt Margaret, and he was besotted with her from the first glance. When he proposed to her, she agreed to the marriage provided she was allowed to continue with her sewing because it afforded her the opportunity to interact with people, which she dearly loved. She was most generous with her time, as well as her wares. If someone admired her work but could not afford to buy it, she would gladly give it to them. The gentry from Durham and York would come to the market in Hartlepool to purchase the tablecloths and napkins she made, and she had quite a list of customers waiting for her to embroider their coat of arms or other sentiments on handkerchiefs. When I was old enough to hold a needle, she taught me how to sew, but she never once insisted I had to. And because she didn't insist, I was always more than happy to help her, even though my skills were far inferior to hers.

"She once told me my brothers and I were the joy of her life. She never rested when one of us was sick but would stay up all night to make sure we were as comfortable as possible. There was never a moment in my life when I doubted her love for me, even when I was obstinate or cross. I miss her horribly even after all these years."

Abby brushed the tears flowing down Colleen's cheek away with the handkerchief that was still in her hand. The touch seemed to bring Colleen back to the present, and she drew in a breath and sat up straight.

"Thank you for sharing your mother with me, Col. How horrible it must have been for you to lose her."

Clasping Abby's hand, Colleen kissed the palm. She raised her head to look into Abby's eyes and whispered, "It was unspeakably tragic indeed. My brothers were taken by the same malady, so it is now just my father and me. I am blessed to have him and wish for you to meet him. And I feel that ... well, you are my family, too. I have never felt closer to another human being, including my mother. Something about you makes me feel I am home when we're together. I don't know if it makes sense, but..."

"Colleen, my beautiful lass, it is as if you can read my mind. When you are not here, my heart aches to be once again in your presence. If you were to say you planned to take me from this place to the most remote corner of the world where we could make a home together, I would ask when we might depart, the sooner to pack my things." Abby laid the handkerchief on the table near the flowers and brushed it flat with her fingers, once again admiring the look of it. She turned back to Colleen and held out her hand to invite her to come closer. Without needing a second invitation, Colleen took the proffered hand and lightly kissed the fingers. Abby's eyes drifted shut at the gentle touch of Colleen's lips. How she'd missed this; there was none other with whom she felt so safe and at the same time so free. Free to be herself, as she had never been with another. "Oh, Col. I've missed you so." She gave voice to the thought she invariably felt upon seeing Colleen walk away after each of their previous meetings.

"And I you. It's good to know you would not be averse to leaving your family to make a home with me. Perhaps one day we can make that happen." She leaned across the table and kissed Abby softly on her lips and was rewarded with a small moan that trembled against her own mouth.

Abby's tongue pressed against her lips lightly, and Colleen opened her mouth to allow her entrance. When at last she broke away to draw a breath, she said, "I can but dream of that day. But for now, I wish to feel your skin under my fingertips. In my mind's eye, I have seen you so many times—the creamy expanses of flesh that must be hidden under the clothes you wear. It's all I can do to restrain myself from tearing them from your body. I know it is a wanton way to behave and hope you do not think less of me."

"How could I think less of you for voicing the exact thoughts that have haunted my mind since the moment we met?" Colleen rose and stepped around the table to stand in front of Abby. Her fingers grasped the leather ties that held her shirt together just below her throat and tugged until the knot was loose. In an almost teasing manner, she drew the ends of the ties free of the fabric until her breasts were exposed. She pulled the shirttails out of her trousers, then allowed the shirt to slide down her arms until her upper body was completely revealed.

To Abby's delight, Colleen wore no corset or other garment beneath her shirt to block her view of the delicious treat before her. "May I touch you then?"

"As you wish, my love. But pray allow me the same pleasure."

"To be sure," Abby said, laughing, "but it will not be so easy to unwrap the package around my gift to you as your own to me. If you will help me…." She rose from her chair and turned her back toward Colleen to give her access to the buttons of her dress. Colleen reached for them immediately.

"Of course. I had plenty of experience helping my mother

with her dress and corsets. I can have you out of this in a trice."
Her skillful fingers made short work of the buttons, then began
to loosen the ties on the corset. As she worked, she sent a silent
message of thanks to her father for not putting his foot down
when she insisted she would no longer wear such garments.
The mere thought of being bound and draped in such finery was
abhorrent to her now. When she removed the corset, her hands
automatically moved to the indentations in Abby's back to rub
them, as she used to do with her mother. But the thought of whose
skin she was touching quickly sent all memories of her mother
into the keepsake box that was her memory of the past. This was
Abby before her, a gift beyond measure, and Colleen felt a chill
creep up her arms that had nothing whatsoever to do with the
temperature in the room.

Abby closed her eyes and leaned back into the hands that
caressed her. Susan was competent enough when it came to
dressing her, but there was never a time when the calloused hands
of her chambermaid touched her in a way to evoke such desire in
her. When Colleen's hands ceased rubbing her back and moved
to her shoulders, Abby turned to face Colleen. Her dress lay in a
heap around her, and her petticoats still hung from her waist, but
her breasts were bare for the first time in the presence of someone
other than a nursemaid, chambermaid, or her mother. She had
to fight her natural inclination to cover the small mounds with
her hands. She was glad she didn't conceal them, for the look in
Colleen's eyes told her more than words ever could, how very
much she loved what she was seeing.

Colleen took one of Abby's hands in her own to steady her
and said, "Step out of the dress and petticoats before you become
entangled in them."

With her free hand, Abby pushed the garments to the floor
and stepped out of them. She stood now mere inches away from
Colleen and could feel the heat radiating off her. When Colleen
released her hand, Abby reached up to touch Colleen's face. "Your
face is flushed. Are you not feeling well?"

"I've never felt better. The flush ... must be caused by another
condition. One that I believe you share." Her fingers grazed over

Abby's cheeks before she leaned down to put her lips against Abby's forehead. "'Tis love, not fever, causing the heat to rise in us, I think."

"I have no basis for comparison, never having felt love such as this before. But, och, lass, I will burn as brightly as Joan of Arc for the pleasure of what I feel now with you." Abby tentatively cupped Colleen's breasts in her hands, noting the solid soft weight that was much greater than her own. Closing her eyes to allow the sense of touch to dominate all others, Abby stroked and kneaded Colleen's breasts before traveling down to her abdomen. When Colleen gasped and her stomach muscles clenched at the touch, Abby opened her eyes to make sure all was still well. The look of pure desire contained in Colleen's eyes reassured her the touch was welcome indeed. Abby grinned wickedly and said, "I only wish you could see the look I see in your eyes, love."

"I'm sure I do. Love, desire, and so much more blaze in your face even brighter than Saint Joan, my darling girl." Wrapping her arms around Abby, she drew her close, unable to bear any further separation. The delicious feel of Abby's skin against hers made her light-headed, and she released her long enough to grasp her hand and lead her toward the couch before she embarrassed herself by collapsing to the floor. Colleen sat down and drew Abby onto her lap. This position placed Abby's breasts within reach of her mouth if Colleen bent her neck slightly, and she was quick to take advantage of the situation. She was not prepared for the immediate hardening of the nipple into something more closely resembling a pebble. Her tongue flicked over it, eliciting moans from Abby, who pressed herself even closer to Colleen. Needing no encouragement, Colleen suckled her breast, then raked the edge of her teeth over the hardened nipple.

Abby's breath caught and she was seized with trembling akin to being naked in a snowstorm. Colleen paused in her suckling to give Abby an inquiring look, but when Abby pulled her head back toward her breast, Colleen smiled and resumed her attention, this time on the other breast.

Abby endured the delicious torture as long as she was able before her need to touch Colleen in a similar fashion forced her to pull back from her lover and rise to her feet. Before Colleen could fully register what had happened, she was pushed backward on the couch and Abby was lying full length on top of her. "My turn," Abby said.

"No arguments from ... oh..." Colleen's voice faded away as Abby buried her face between Colleen's breasts, kissing and licking from one to the other.

Abby believed firmly in turnabout being fair play, and she lavished as much attention as she could on Colleen's breasts before curiosity drove her to explore further. Straddling Colleen's hips, her hands traced the tips of her ribs before dipping down to touch the smooth belly. She marveled once again at how a mere touch could cause the muscles there to contract. Returning her attention to the tantalizing globes, she pinched the nipples between her fingers until Colleen moaned.

Colleen's eyes were closed, her head thrown back. She began to writhe underneath her lover. None of the tales of lovemaking she'd overheard her shipmates bragging about prepared her for the exquisite torture Abby's touch supplied. Intellectually, she understood the mechanics of it, but clearly that was a very small part of the equation. Love was the ingredient that made the difference, she surmised.

Abby sank down on top of Colleen once again. She kissed her deeply once, then trailed kisses down her neck to her chest. She began a slow descent kissing and licking as she went, dipping her tongue into Colleen's navel before reaching the trousers that prevented further exploration. She reached for the cord keeping the trousers in place, but her hand was stopped by Colleen's gentle touch. She turned her curious gaze on her lover, who tugged on her arms and motioned for her to come and lie down upon her breast again. "But I want—"

"Shh, love. When the time is right, we'll take the next steps. I don't want our first time to be rushed, and I fear I need to get back to the ship soon."

Abby looked at Colleen with incredulity before finally crawling up to lay her head upon the soft breast she longed to feast upon again. "Colleen, you are a beast. Every nerve in my body is screaming. I feel as if I might explode, and you say you need to get back to the ship. If I didn't love you so much, I would slap you."

Colleen chuckled. "Abby, I think I can calm those nerves for you, if you'll allow me, only pray don't beat on me."

"And just what are you thinking you might—"

Before Abby could complete her thought, Colleen slipped out from under her and sat up, pulling Abby close and raining kisses upon her face. She trailed her hand down Abby's body until she reached the spot so desperately craving her attention. With soft strokes, she parted the folds to expose the bundle of nerves she was all too familiar with from exploration of her own body. At the first touch, Abby's body jerked and stiffened; clearly, she had never been touched before. Colleen pulled her hand away long enough to tilt Abby's face to her. She kissed her on the cheek and whispered, "Fear not, I won't hurt you."

Abby's skin felt as if she had been bitten by a swarm of ants, only there was no discomfort involved, only a most pleasant tingle. When Colleen whispered in her ear, Abby nodded and relaxed somewhat, unable to make a verbal reply for the moment but clearly not opposed to what Colleen was doing.

"Have you ever brought pleasure to yourself with your hands, Abby?" When Abby shook her head no, Colleen said, "I'm going to show you how you can do that for yourself when I'm not here. Relax—close your eyes and just feel how I touch you."

Abby closed her eyes and tried her best to relax, but the way Colleen was touching her made it most difficult. As Colleen's fingers trailed lightly over Abby's abdomen, Abby couldn't help but twitch. When Colleen reached the apex of her legs, Abby moaned outright. And her mind danced with a thousand thoughts, chiefly that what Colleen was doing was the most pleasant experience she'd ever had. That it was a shame she had not discovered this pleasure much earlier in her life flit briefly across her consciousness, but it was overridden by her gratitude that Colleen, whom she loved, was introducing her to these delicious pleasures.

With feather-light touches, Colleen circled Abby's clitoris, only brushing against it every few strokes to avoid overstimulating her inexperienced lover. Taking her cue from Abby's breathing, which changed to short gasps, Colleen picked up the tempo, putting more forceful touches upon Abby's clitoris. "That's it, Abby. You feel it building, don't you?"

"Oh, Colleen, yes…" Abby's eyes were tightly shut, and her body was taut. She lifted up to meet Colleen's hand to prolong the contact. She was not sure what was about to happen, but she knew it would be wonderful because it was Colleen who gave it to her.

"Let yourself go, love. I've got you."

Abby felt as if her body exploded into tiny fragments and gradually rained down upon the couch. "I am … undone, Col. What sorcery have you worked upon me?"

"Not sorcery, precious one. It's called 'the little death,'" Colleen said with a grin. Since she had never tried to give an orgasm to anyone but herself, she was uncertain as to whether she could truly accomplish her goal. The look on Abby's face gave her the answer.

Lacking bones with which to move from where she lay, Abby simply let her head drop to one side, where it came into contact with Colleen's breast. With a sigh, she said, "It's a shame only men and babies get to sample these delights."

Colleen laughed. "Not such a shame. Mine are yours for the taking. It's the timing that's not right. I wish to make love to you for hours, please you beyond your wildest dreams. We have only a scrap of time this day."

"But when shall we find that kind of time? Our moments are stolen ones, and you are here so seldom. I can't imagine how I'm going to survive until the next time." Tears ran down Abby's cheeks and onto Colleen's breast. Colleen brushed them off with her thumb and kissed Abby's forehead.

"Five months at most I will return. I will contrive a reason for us to stay here more than the usual two or three days, and if you can come up with an excuse to absent yourself from your duties, perhaps we can have the time we both desire most ardently."

Abby sighed. "Five long months, indeed. I shall watch for the blue scarf every day starting four months from today."

"We have a bargain then. And now I fear we must compose ourselves and go back to our—"

"Dreary lives," Abby finished with a pout on her face. But she knew Colleen was right; this was not their moment, much as she wished it so. The likelihood of anyone coming to the boathouse was slim, but if a chance was there at all, they could not risk discovery. She had escaped the suitors her mother pressed upon her from time to time, but she knew she could not hope to continue to do so if her love for Colleen were exposed. Rising from the couch, she took up her corset from where it lay on the floor and handed it to Colleen. "Make it tight, Col. Susan is ruthless when tying this dreadful thing, and she'll know it's been removed if it's not strangling me." Colleen pulled the laces tight, but Abby shook her head to show they should be tighter still. "And none of your fancy nautical knots either, lass ... oof." Abby was nearly pulled off her feet by the last tug, and breath was hard to draw. "That's Susan's way, right enough."

After Colleen finished dressing Abby, she pulled her own shirt on. The look on Abby's face as her breasts were covered nearly broke her heart. She pulled Abby into her arms and whispered, "We must be strong until the day we can be together forever. We are resourceful and clever women. Without a doubt we shall find a way. Now show me a smile before I leave. I can't bear for this sad look to be the one I carry with me to sea."

Abby did her best to smile, and even though the ends of her mouth turned up, her eyes belied the attempt. She took a breath at last and finally found a true smile to bestow upon Colleen. "Please tell me that when we clever women are together, I need no longer wear corsets. How I envy you your freedom."

"Your comfort is my greatest wish," Colleen said. "Now I beg you, kiss me with enough ardor to last us both until five months hence."

Abby drew Colleen's head down and kissed her until she thought she might faint. "I trust that will last for five months, but not a day more. Please come back to me then. I am not whole without you."

"Nor I, you. I shall be here then, my love." Fearing she might cry if she continued to gaze into Abby's sad eyes, Colleen walked to the door and stepped out into the fading moments of a brilliant sunset.

Pirates

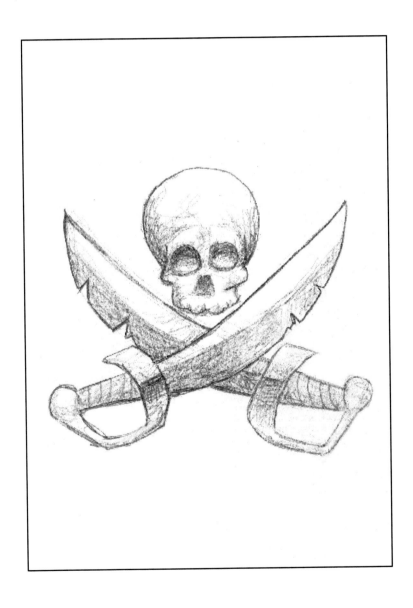

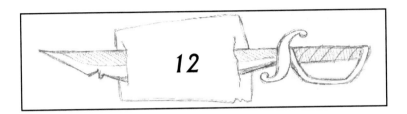

The Caribbean, 1717

"Here are your choices, lads." Jack Rackham paced the deck of the newly acquired sloop *William*, obtained during a mutiny against the English captain of the vessel. Strolling to the railing, he glanced over the side, and with a chuckle, he said, "You may join your captain on his long trip to the bottom of the sea. Or you can join me and my mates here and become rich. Bear in mind, I can run this ship with half of you, and I have no problem tossing you over the side. So step forward if you're with me, boys."

Among the sailors was Mary Read, known on board as Mark Read. She'd been among the pirates to take advantage of King George's pardon and had lived a fairly uneventful life in the Bahamas for nearly a year before signing on with a privateer commissioned to protect the British interests from the Spaniards. And now, on her first voyage, she was being pressed once again into piracy. With a shrug, she stepped forward. "I'm with you, Calico. I ain't much of a swimmer."

The remainder of the crew mumbled their agreement with Read, and Jack—known as Calico Jack because of his colorful striped pants—clapped her on the back nearly hard enough to send her sprawling to the deck. "Clever boy, Read. There's a fortune for the taking in these waters, and I aim to get my share." A natural born leader, he assigned tasks to his crew and soon the sloop was underway toward Port Royal in Jamaica where he planned to take on supplies.

From her hiding place in the forecastle, Anne Bonny watched as Read went about his chores. Anne believed, as did the rest of the crew, that Read was a male. And she was attracted to Read for the gentleness that separated him from the rest of the men. Dressing in men's clothing only to simplify the work she had to do, Anne did not hide her gender from her shipmates. All but the most recent additions to the crew knew not only that she was a woman, but also that she belonged to Calico Jack. None would dare approach her even if they'd taken a fancy to her. Only now it was she who had taken a fancy to one of the new lads, and she was not quite sure what to do about it. Jack's temper was well known, and if she pursued something with Read and it got back to him, the young sailor's life expectancy would be short indeed.

Mary was not unaware of Anne's surveillance. Several times, she'd caught the Irish lass sneaking surreptitious glances at her while she was about her chores, but Anne always quickly looked away or showed an air of indifference when Mary's eyes met her own. Having passed as a male for most of her life, Mary was not unfamiliar with the pleasures to be had in the arms of a woman. She normally kept her own gender hidden from her sexual partners by employing artificial devices to simulate the missing male parts or through the skillful use of her fingers and tongue, and she was almost always rewarded by praise of the highest order. She fancied herself quite the lover. A tumble with the fiery redheaded lass would be lovely as long as the pirate captain's suspicions were not aroused. She meant it when she said she was not much of a swimmer.

"Read, give us a hand." Mary stopped and turned at the sound of Anne's voice and found her attempting to sort out the foresail line, which was hopelessly tangled with the jib line.

"Oh, right." Mary was returning to her bunk after emptying her slop bucket over the side. She stashed the bucket in a nook in the forecastle, then took up the end of one of the ropes to unwind it. "How in hell did this get so buggered up?" she muttered under her breath.

Anne simply shrugged and began to work at the tangle from the other end. Of course she'd arranged the knots herself and lain in wait for Read to come by to have an excuse to talk with the sailor, who now occupied the majority of her waking thoughts. "I've no idea, I'm sure. But we'll not get these sails aloft with this mess, for a fact." As Anne worked, she drew closer to Mary, who had very nearly completed her task.

When Mary looked up, she found Anne standing so close she could hear her breath over the sounds of the waves parting before the hull of the ship. Their fingers touched as the last knot was undone and the rope dropped to the deck.

"Meet me in the hold by the capstan after yer shift is done," Anne whispered so her voice would not carry to the sailors in the forecastle working to raise the sails. Mary simply nodded, and Anne said, "Good lad. I'll be waiting."

Mary watched as Anne made her way toward the main deck. "Oh, and alas, what have I got meself into now?" Mary said as she collected her slop bucket and made her way once again to her bunk to stow it with the rest of her gear.

Jack was snoring loudly enough to wake the former captain of the *William* from his watery grave. Anne slid out of his bunk silently and pulled her dressing gown on to cover her naked form. Jack insisted she sleep in the nude, and she found it rather suited her, except on those occasions when she was not in the mood and he forced himself upon her. Alas, those incidents were happening more and more often, and Anne sometimes wished she could simply walk away and never look back. Unfortunately, they were at sea, and there was nowhere to go. Jack's snores stopped the moment Anne stepped to the floor, and she stood stock-still until the unearthly sounds once again issued from his still form. She'd heard snores before, but none was the equal of Calico Jack's. Anne crept to the door of the stateroom and slowly opened it, thankful she'd noticed the squeak in the door earlier in the day and had given it a generous dousing with oil. She glanced up and down the hallway and found nobody stirring, which is what she would have expected at such a late hour. Tying the sash of her robe tightly about her waist, she made her way to the hatch leading down to the hold where she planned to meet up with the intriguing Mark Read.

Mary lounged against the wall of the hold, her ears alert for any sounds from upside indicating the approach of the Irish lass. Her eyes were accustomed to the dark, and she knew she'd be able to tell if someone, other than Anne, came down the stairs and it was necessary for her to hide. Mary had secreted a small phallus inside her trousers, attached to her leg with a leather thong. She had fashioned the device herself using a smooth piece of wood wrapped in cloth to ensure it was not so hard as to hurt and covering it off with a soft layer of kid skin. In the dark, it would be simple to convince Anne it was the real thing.

At the sound of the creaking of the hatch door, Mary crouched back into the shadows, all but invisible from anyone above. She saw first one, then another shapely feminine leg descend the stairs, and with a grin, Mary pushed away from the wall to intercept her. Grasping her waist, she lowered Anne to the floor.

"Oh!"

"Shh. Somebody might hear you."

At the sound of Read's voice, Anne relaxed and rapped Mary sharply on the arm. "You frightened me within an inch of me life, you brute." The tone of her voice did not match the words as she pressed her body up against Mary's, her knee working its way between her strong thighs. Mary pulled back slightly to ensure the phallus remained fixed against her thigh, and at the same time bent to kiss Anne softly, hoping the withdrawal would be construed as a wish to draw out the pleasure of their first encounter, rather than the desire to distance herself from her companion. Anne's eyes closed and she sighed as Mary's lips withdrew. The kiss was as sensual and exciting as anything she had experienced. Worlds removed from the wet sloppy kisses of the pirate captain snoring in his cabin.

"Raise up a bit," Mary said when she came up for air. When Anne complied, Mary dragged over a pallet she'd made from some of the bales of Indian cloth that Jack planned on using to turn into even more colorful pants. It seemed fitting his woman should get some pleasure out of the fabric, as well. After Anne settled back down, Mary whispered, "Does this meet with your approval, my lady?"

Anne laughed. "I can't see a thing, Read. It's dark as the hinges of hell itself in here. But if you say it's good, then I'm for it."

Mary smiled. Everything was going as she hoped. She grasped the ties holding Anne's dressing gown together and gave a tug, gasping softly at the large smooth breasts revealed when the fabric fell open. Mary was glad her eyes had adjusted to the dim light as the sight before her made her mouth fairly water.

"I'm guessing from your sounds you like what you see."

Mary nodded, then realized Anne could not see the nod. "Oh, it's lovely indeed. A shame all these curves must be hidden behind clothing so much of the time." She lowered her head to take a breast into her mouth and suckled greedily. Her teeth lightly nipped at the hardening nipple, and Anne groaned and sagged in her arms. Mary released her hold on the breast upon which she was feasting to lower Anne to the pallet. She dropped down beside her and resumed her attentions upon the enticing globes before her. First one, then the other were suckled and kneaded until Anne began to writhe and moan underneath her.

Through gritted teeth, Anne said, "Read, if you don't touch me between me legs very soon, I shall be forced to take matters into me own hands."

"No rush, my lady. I shall get there in time. All the better for the anticipation, I hope." Mary squeezed Anne's ample breasts, pinching the nipples until Anne moaned once again and took hold of Mary's hand, dragging it down her belly toward the place most craving attention.

"Please, I beg you, no more teasing. I suspect yer more than ready yerself," Anne whispered huskily. Before Mary could do anything to stop it, Anne's hand fell on her thigh and came into contact with the phallus through the fabric of her trousers. Taking it to be her swelling manhood, Anne gave it a squeeze, only to have it come loose in her hand. She jerked her hand away as if it had been burned. "What in the—!"

Mary clamped her hand quickly over Anne's mouth before she could rouse others on the ship with her noise. "Please, keep your voice down. I shall explain, but we'll both be flogged or worse if Jack finds us here. Will you be quiet if I take my hand away?" Anne nodded, and Mary removed her hand.

The fiery Irish woman smacked her once again on the shoulder, having regained her senses enough to be angry at being deceived. And if truth be told, she was near to bursting with sexual excitement and only wished Read could finish what he ... she ... started. "Just tell me, are you a woman?"

"Yes, but—"

"Damn yer eyes." Anne made as if to rise from the pallet, jerking her dressing gown back over her shoulders.

"Wait! I promise you I can do what any man can do, and better, if you'll but allow me to continue."

"Can you now?" Anne scoffed, but she relaxed back onto the pallet willing at least to find out if Read could do as she seemed to think she could.

"Yes, I can. I know what pleases a woman, how to touch her." Her hand began to caress the exposed flesh of Anne's belly with feather-light touches, raising goose flesh in their wake. "And I know what excites her and makes her want to scream." She covered Anne's lips with her own, her tongue entreating entrance to Anne's mouth. Anne's own tongue met Mary's tentatively at first, then with more enthusiasm. Without a doubt, Read's kisses were the most skilled she'd ever experienced. Perhaps the rest of her boasts were equally true.

"None has ever made me want to scream except with the desire to be as far away as possible from themselves," Anne said when Mary broke the kiss to straddle the Irish woman with her legs.

"This is a completely different scream," Mary promised as she kissed her way down the length of Anne's body. "You might want to ... put a bit of cloth in your mouth to stifle the sound, or you'll wake the entire ship."

"Awful sure of yerself, eh, bucko?" She sounded skeptical but nevertheless grabbed a handful of cloth and pulled it toward her face when Mary's tongue parted the folds of her womanhood. No man had ventured there with his tongue before, content merely to thrust himself upon her until he spent his seed. This was a new experience and thrilling beyond what she had felt before. She shuddered as Mary's tongue found the hardening button of flesh longing for attention.

"Very sure. Stop talking and just feel what I'm doing."

"Oh, yes." And when she realized she was still talking, she stuffed the cloth firmly in her mouth to prevent further words from escaping during the experience.

Mary brought her tongue up the underside of Anne's clitoris and felt it quiver. To prolong Anne's pleasure, she moved down farther to her opening and thrust her tongue inside, feeling the soft velvety walls contract as if to keep her there. Removing the phallus from inside her pants, she brought the rounded end of it up to join her tongue and heard the "Oh!" Anne could not suppress with an entire bolt of cloth. Mary rolled the phallus up and down the opening until it was entirely wet, then slipped it inside. By then, Anne was writhing almost uncontrollably, her hips rising off the floor. Mary returned to the stiff clitoris and sucked it into her mouth while slowly working the phallus in and out.

Anne began to suspect the scream Read talked about had more to do with unmerciful teasing, and she very nearly removed the cloth from her mouth to ask nicely if Read would bloody get on with it, when her orgasm began to build. Never had she experienced anything as intense as this. The phallus within her was touching a spot few men had been able to find even in good light. And Read's tongue ... ah, that tongue had magic in it without a doubt. The promised scream was torn from her throat, and Anne turned her head to muffle the cry against her own shoulder. Rational thought fled as she raised her body so far off the pallet she very nearly knocked Mary from her perch. But Mary held on tenaciously until Anne finally fell back to the floor, one hand attempting to stop Mary from continuing the delicious torture while the other drew the cloth from her mouth.

"Oh, stop ... please. I beg you. I can't take any more of this.

You win. You spoke the truth about your skills. I shall not doubt
you again. Only please tell me we can do this again—and soon.
Perhaps you can teach me some of the tricks you do with your
tongue so I might bring some of this pleasure to you, as well"

Mary rolled onto her side, a self-satisfied smile on her face.
"Oh, lass, be sure we'll do this again. And I would consider it
an honor to teach you some of my tricks. But for now, you must
return to Jack's bed before he misses you. And I must ... er, take
care of my own needs." She wiggled her fingers in the air.

"Perhaps I could do it for you. I have more than a little
experience in bringing meself pleasure when me bed mate rolled
over and began to snore." She pushed herself up on one elbow and
leaned over Mary as if to kiss her, but Mary pulled away.

"Nay, not a good idea. It's not unusual for a woman to bear
the smell of herself upon her hand because of the need to satiate
a hunger. But if you kiss me, you will have the smell of yourself
upon your face. A bit harder to explain. Another time, perhaps,
when we have thought to bring water and soap to remove the
evidence."

"As you say, bucko. You know more than I about such things.
But I do want to touch you ... pleasure you." Her hands found the
sash binding Mary's pants and loosened it. "Raise up," she said,
and Mary complied, allowing Anne to pull the garment down her
legs. She wore no undergarments, and the proof of her excitement
glistened on the lips of her sex, evident even in the almost non-
existent light.

Hesitantly at first, Anne began to finger the slick folds,
tentatively pushing a finger inside the tight hole, which opened
like a flower at her touch. "You won't hurt me," Mary whispered.
"Touch me harder.... Yes, like that."

Anne warmed to the task as Mary began to buck underneath
her fingers. She knew from her own experience she should soon
begin to put more pressure on the swelling nub of flesh, but she
was reluctant to end the lesson too soon. Instead she pushed
one finger firmly inside and felt the silken walls close in around
her as if to hold her there forever. Her thumb found the clitoris
and massaged it slowly until the urgent jerking of Read's body

beneath her told her she must allow her to climax or explain the presence of a nearly naked dead female sailor in the hold to the very possessive Jack Rackham.

"Please, please, please," Mary whispered like a mantra, and upon hearing the desperation in her voice, Anne put pressure more directly on the clitoris. "Yes ... yes ... oh, God, yes!" The orgasm began and rolled over Mary's body in seemingly never-ending waves.

Anne crawled on top of Mary and lay down, her own ample breasts nearly crushing the bound breasts of her companion. Mary's heartbeat thundered so wildly in her chest, the feeling reverberated in Anne's chest, as well. Mary's breath came in ragged gasps that slowly returned to normal. "Tell me, sailor, what do they call you at home?"

"I was christened Mary, but my mother called me Mark from the time I was small. But that's a story for another time."

"Ah, me mother's name was Mary, a grand old name. And our secret, Mary Read."

"Yes. Our secret."

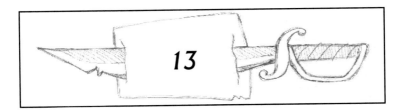

Mary and Anne devised a system of signals to indicate when they might be able to get away from their tasks for more of what they both decided was the most pleasurable sex they'd ever had. Mary was the boatswain in charge of the ships rigging, and when she wished to let Anne know she would be free, she would tie backward knots in the rigging—one knot for each hour until she would be able to sneak away to their secret spot in the hold. If Anne was unable to keep the engagement, she would untie the knots and replace them with one properly tied knot and one backward knot. If any of the other sailors wondered at the odd way the boatswain tied knots, none of them said anything. Read seemed to be a favorite with Calico, and none of his shipmates wished to risk his disfavor by pointing out the peculiar behavior of the boatswain.

One early morning just over a month after their initial rendezvous, Mary found Anne lying upon the pallet when she arrived in the hold. The smells were worse than the normal odors of rotting cargo, which was an everyday part of a sailor's life. The smell of sickness hung in the air, as well. When her eyes adjusted sufficiently to allow her to navigate the cluttered area, she saw the bucket near Anne's head from which the rank odor emanated.

"What ails you, love?" Mary asked, kneeling down to brush her fingers across Anne's forehead. Seasickness was a common cause of a sailor's discomfort, but the seas were entirely calm that dark morning just before daybreak. Something else must be the cause of her stomach distress.

"Oh, and I wish I knew. It come upon me just after I slipped out of Jack's bunk to make me way down here. I was lucky to lay me hands upon a bucket before I made a mess on deck."

"I warned you about eating that salamagundi Hawkins cooked up. I always go hungry when he's the one doing the cooking."

"Nay, I did not eat it. 'Tis something else ailing me. For several days now I've wakened with..." Her voice broke off and her eyes widened as she realized what it might be. "Bloody hell." She grabbed Mary's hand and tugged her nearly off balance as she clutched it to her chest. "Do you remember—since we've been keeping company—have I been plagued with the woman's curse?"

"Never, to my recollection, but we only ... oh, God, are you with child? I thought you'd not been with Jack since we—"

"Not of my own accord." Anne's voice showed a trace of bitterness Mary had not heard before. "Sometimes he has his way with me whether I wish it or not. I hate to think what he'll do when he learns of it. Oh, Mary, what shall I do?"

It was so unlike Anne to call her by her given name that Mary was quiet for a moment before she sat down and drew Anne's head into her lap. "Shh, love, don't let it worry you over much. We shall think of something, the two of us."

Anne sat up intending to thank Mary for being there for her when her belly was seized with pain, and she leaned over to retch into her bucket once again.

Mary held Anne's hair back to keep it from falling into the bucket and hummed a childhood lullaby her own mother had crooned to her in the hope it would comfort her friend. This was going to be a challenge, no mistake.

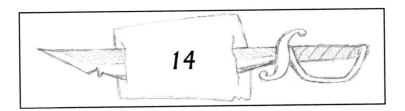

Two months after the successful mutiny, the *William* pulled into Nassau intending to take on fresh water and foodstuffs. Anne told Jack she needed some "women's" potions and planned to visit the apothecary while the crew took on supplies. He was intent upon the lists of items he was going over and dismissed her with a wave. Mary deliberately delayed her departure from the ship until she saw Anne nod to let her know she should follow, but as previously discussed, she left enough time for Anne to be out of sight before disembarking.

Anne was engaged in conversation with the chemist when Mary entered the shop. Without wishing to be intrusive, but at the same time showing her support for this woman of whom she had become inordinately fond during the past two months, Mary retreated to a corner where the myriad smells were least offensive and pretended to be interested in a mortar and pestle.

The chemist reached to a shelf behind the counter and pulled out a burlap sack filled with a riotous assortment of leaves. Placing it on the counter, he moved a stool to a shelf where he reached into an earthen jar and took out a piece of root of some sort. Mary could not make out much of their conversation, but she did hear that the root had come from the colonies, as if the very distance it had traveled had imparted it with some magical powers. The chemist removed a fist-sized bunch of leaves from the burlap sack and laid them out on a block of cloth, tying the cloth in a bundle. The root he handed to Anne and gestured for her to put it in her purse. Apparently, the two ingredients did not want to be transported together. Anne pulled some coins from her purse and handed them to the chemist, then turning with her purchases, she made her way to the door. As she was about to reach for the handle, the door opened and a well-dressed young woman stood without, a somewhat older woman dressed in the simple garments of a housemaid, or some such servant, standing just behind her. Anne and the young woman jumped back a bit, each surprised to encounter the other.

"Oh, pardon me," the young woman said, backing away from the door to allow Anne to exit and very nearly knocking into the servant behind her.

Several very colorful retorts sprung to Anne's mind, but before she gave voice to them, she looked the woman over carefully. The dress she wore was British-made if she was not mistaken, and jewels hung around her neck on a golden chain. Everything about her spoke of wealth and station. There was money to be made here if a body were to snatch up the little tart.

Anne stepped back from the door and dropped a curtsy to the lady, grateful that for this particular outing, she was wearing her women's clothes. "No, my lady, 'tis I should be begging your pardon. I should've looked before barreling through the door. Please, come inside."

Mary saw the entire exchange from the corner where she stood, and as the young woman entered the shop, she also took stock of her. Anne caught Mary's eye as the woman approached the counter. The chemist had apparently been expecting her because he fetched a jar from the shelf and set it on the counter with a smile. "Good morning to you, Miss Hume. I pray your mother is not in immediate need of these powders." Anne knew the governor was named Hume and presumed this young noblewoman to be his daughter. With a jerk of her head and a few hand gestures, Anne indicated for Mary to keep the woman in her sight until she could fetch some reinforcements. Mary nodded and leaned back against the wall to see what would happen next.

Abby favored the apothecary with a smile that lit up even the corner where Mary stood. The lady was beautiful as well as wealthy, and no mistake. "Good morning, Mr. Donovan. She is well at the moment but very nearly out of her headache powder, and you know how she worries if she doesn't have a generous supply on hand. I'm grateful to you for making this up for me on such short notice."

"Be sure I would drop anything I might be working on to take care of the wife of the governor. Your mother is my best customer, Miss Hume." He noted the amount to be charged for the powders on a ledger with the governor's seal on the cover.

"I know she is, Mr. Donovan, and I wish she didn't suffer so." Then she leaned closer and whispered to him conspiratorially, "Though I suspect many of her headaches are due to the pressures she is under as wife of the governor. I don't think she realized how much would be expected of her here in the islands."

"Aye. In this part of the world, she's as close as you can get to a queen. And you, of course, to a princess." He smiled and bowed.

Mary smiled as her mind calculated the amount of gold the governor would pay to recover his little princess. The pirates she had sailed with before preferred to capture booty rather than people. The reward was more immediate, and you didn't have to feed and care for a chest full of gold. But she knew Jack would be happy to feed and care for such a lovely captive if the prize were great enough.

Mary watched from the door as the lady and her maid left the apothecary and entered a shop a bit farther down the lane. She followed at a respectful distance, then stopped in front of the shop next door to it. She knew she would stand out as an oddity in a dressmaker's shop, so she pretended to study the display in the window of the green grocer. With a glance, she could see if the lady exited the shop and, at the same time, be able to see reflected in the window the lane from which Anne and the reinforcements would come.

It seemed hours had passed during which time Mary studied every item displayed in the window of the grocer until she knew each one by heart. She could swear mold started to grow on a chunk of cheese in the time she stood there, and she only hoped she had not aroused suspicion from either the shopkeeper or passers-by due to her interest in the shop's contents. She glanced up at the sound of the bell on the dressmaker's door to see the lady and her maid emerge. There was no sign of Anne coming down the lane, so Mary was loath to leave the area for fear her crew would not be able to find their quarry if they were no longer near the shops. As Abby approached the spot where she stood, Mary reached into her pocket and withdrew a gold coin, which she tossed to the ground at the young noblewoman's feet.

"Pardon, Miss, but I believe you've dropped a coin." Mary hurried to recover the coin and held it in front of the lady, who stopped rather than run into the seaman who blocked her path.

"Nay, good sir, I carry no coin. 'Tis not mine." Mary's eyes met the young woman's for just an instant, and in the brief flicker of time that elapsed, she suspected the governor's daughter realized she was a woman.

Abby gave Mary a brief smile as she hooked her arm through her maid's but made only one step forward before the maid stopped short. Hefting her purse as if to weigh its contents, the maid turned toward Mary and said, "I believe it's mine, sir. I have discovered a hole in my purse." Abby looked at the maid with something bordering on incredulity, Mary thought, but the noblewoman said nothing.

"Ah, are you sure now?" Mary said, pulling the coin out of reach of the maid and pretending to study it. She had counted upon the lady to be honest, and the maid to be silent, as was usually the case in the upper classes. She could ill afford to lose the money and scrambled to come up with a reason why it could not belong to the maid. "This is a Dutch Ducat, a fair bit of money for one ... such as yourself."

"The governor himself give it to me, sir."

"I assure you, sir, Susan is not in the habit of lying," Abby said, the Scottish lilt in her voice giving a delightful trill to the word "sir" and sending a tiny chill up Mary's back. Despite her words, Mary could tell by the look on Abby's face she was not altogether certain the coin had, in fact, been given to her maid by the governor. When Susan held her hand out, Mary had no option but to give her the coin. With a sigh, she dropped it in the maid's hand and watched as her hard-earned spoils disappeared inside her purse.

"Then it's glad I am to help restore it to its rightful owner, miss. I am pleased to have been of assistance to a lady as lovely as yourself." Mary took Susan's hand and lightly brushed her lips over the knuckles, noting as she raised her head to look once again in Susan's face, the blush that crept up her cheeks. Whether it was from the kiss or from the out-and-out lie she told, Mary could not guess.

"Come along, Susan. Mother will be having fits as it is we've been gone so long." Abby took one step, but before she could take another, Mary had side-stepped in front of her to block her passage. Abby stood up tall and looked Mary in the eye. "Kindly let me pass, sir."

"I wish only to apologize for my rudeness, miss. I hope you will forgive this humble sailor for doubting the word of such a lady as yourself for even one moment." She bowed and reached for Abby's hand, bestowing the same soft kiss upon it as she had upon the maid's. When she rose once again to look in the noblewoman's eyes, she saw something there ... recognition, perhaps? Glancing over Abby's shoulder, Mary saw Anne, Jack, and several crewmen approaching down the lane. With an almost imperceptible jerk of her head, she indicated they should continue past the shops and into the alley behind. From there, they could follow Mary's progress until they could snatch the prize without witnesses present. "Allow me to safely escort you home, my lady. I've heard there be pirates in port these days." She took Abby's elbow and began to steer her down the boardwalk. Susan trailed a respectable several steps behind as they walked along, her fingers tracing the outline of the unexpected good fortune within her purse.

"Oh, you're just trying to frighten me. Truly, I need no escort.

Susan and I frequently come into town alone, and we have always been perfectly safe. Surely you have better things to do than—"

"Believe me, miss. I have seen the ship myself. The *William* is in port, proud as you please, flying the flag of Calico Jack."

"I … I have heard of him. A vicious cutthroat, so they say."

"Aye, 'tis the scuttlebutt. A very good man to avoid, and no mistake."

"Then I'm grateful to you, sir, for your assistance. Please tell me, what vessel brings you to our shores?"

Mary cast about for the name of a vessel she knew to be in port, as well, and remembered one bearing part of the name of her shipmate and lover. "The *Betsy Ann*, miss. Aye, that's the one." She was surprised when Abby stopped in her tracks and wheeled on her. Mary very nearly collided with her, so surprised was she at the abrupt halt.

"Colleen is here? I had no idea. Has she gone to my father's house? We must hurry. I do not want to miss her again. Susan, please hurry ahead and bring the carriage here straight away. I..." The curious look on Susan's face stopped the excited words from tumbling from her mouth. Quickly, she added, "She's an old friend from home. I have not seen her in a long time, and we have so much to catch up on. We mustn't delay, Susan." Abby took hold of Susan's arm and propelled her in the direction of the stable where the carriage waited for them.

Taking advantage of Abby's obvious excitement coupled with her apparent distress at the thought of failing to meet up with the seemingly lucky Colleen, Mary quickly said, "No, miss, she has not gone to your father's house right off. She said she was going to stop at the ... uh, Fox and Hound Tavern first for a pint. If we hurry along between these buildings, we may intercept her before she leaves. Miss Susan, your mistress may need to have the carriage meet her elsewhere, so please come along with us." Susan turned around and looked to Abby for further directions.

"Yes, please, Susan, come with us. When we find Colleen, we shall decide what to do."

Mary shepherded them along until they reached the alley where she knew her shipmates to be. She could see several forms hurrying just ahead of them, so she spoke in a loud voice to make sure they knew she was coming with the prize and would take measures not to be seen until she and Abby were upon them. "The tavern is just up here a bit, miss. Watch your step, there's some foul business that'll make a ruin of your gown." Abby raised the hem of her dress and studied the ground before her but saw nothing. When she looked up again, she saw several well-armed men forming a line and blocking the alley. Instinctively, she reached out for the arm of the sailor who promised to protect her, only to find he had fallen behind and was holding Susan's arms to prevent her from running away. Abby opened her mouth to cry for help and found a filthy hand clamped over her mouth and an arm wrapped firmly around her waist. She bit down on the hand, and it was jerked away, but only long enough to make a fist, which hit her in the jaw. Her knees sagged, and the only thing keeping her up was the arm around her waist. After a moment, she shook her head and regained her footing, only to have a foul-tasting bandanna shoved in her mouth and tied around her head. Her hands were roughly pulled behind her and quickly tied. She was hauled off her feet, which were also bound, and the rope looped through the one around her wrists, effectively preventing her from kicking as one of the men heaved her up over his shoulder.

"Miserable git took a hunk outta me hand," one of the men groused.

"Sod your hand, Gunny," Jack said. "You can buy enough rum to drown out the pain in your hand with the prize from this haul." He made his way to where Mary still held a trembling Susan captive, and grasping her chin in his hand, he looked her straight in the eye. "Listen good, love, 'cause your mistress's life depends on it. Tell the governor to bring a thousand pounds or fifteen hundred doubloons, it matters not a whit to me, to the Hog's Breath Tavern in Port Royal in a week to retrieve his lovely daughter. Tell him Calico Jack gives his word she will be untouched if he does as I say, but if not, he might expect to receive her back in pieces ... not all at once, mind. Got that, love?" Susan nodded, and Jack patted her cheek. "Good girl. Now you just stay here with Read for a bit until we have a chance to get this little lovely on board ship, then take yourself home. And remember ... Hog's Breath Tavern. Oh, and tell him to leave the Royal Navy at home, eh?" Jack tossed a length of rope at Mary's feet and indicated with a nod that Susan should be prevented from going home for quite a while. Mary acknowledged his instructions with a wink.

Mary watched the progress of her shipmates until they were out of sight. She turned the servant girl so she could see her face but did not loosen her grip on Susan's arms. "Let's have that purse of yours, lass. You have something belonging to me." She carefully fished only the Ducat out of the purse before handing it back to Susan, who glared at her openly. "Honor among thieves, m'dear. I only took the one you stole from me. Now so you don't make it home before we can get underway, I would be obliged if you would give me your hands." When Susan complied, Mary wound the rope around her wrists and tied a loose knot, not wishing to hurt her. Ducking into an alley populated only by shadows, Mary dragged her captive to where it was dark enough for her to be invisible from either end of the alley. She then threaded the rope through an iron ring intended for tying horses and made a sturdier knot. "That should hold you for a bit. Now ... to keep you quiet. Ah…" She untied the apron Susan wore, rolled it into an effective gag, and tied it around her head. When she was satisfied Susan would remain undiscovered until the ship was well away, Mary planted a kiss on the top of Susan's head, and with a small wave, she set out to join her shipmates and their latest prize.

"Damn yer eyes, woman!" Anne roared, clutching her throbbing shin, which had been soundly kicked by the struggling noblewoman. "I'll give you twice what for if you so much as touch me again."

"How dare you threaten me! My father is the governor and the lord of—"

"I know who yer bleedin' father is, you silly git. It's why we grabbed you. We'll fetch a pretty penny from his lordship for your safe return. But I vow, I would just as soon gut you as look at you, so you might want to just settle down and not give me reason to do so, eh?" The pirate lass maintained a healthy distance as she looped a length of rope around the still-kicking legs and tugged until they were immobile against the legs of the chair upon which Abby sat. "That ought to hold you for a while, yer grace. If yer lucky, one of the lads might bring you something to eat ... sometime. And keep yer feet to yerself. Not all these lads are as gentle as meself." Without a backward glance, Anne made her way to the steps leading out of the hold and climbed up, dropping the hatch door behind her, leaving Abby in the dark.

Abby struggled against her bonds but was unable to make any headway. She could feel her heartbeat accelerate and her breathing begin to labor, and she tried unsuccessfully to calm herself down. "Please!" she shouted into the dark. "Free my hands at least so I might fend off any creatures that would harm me." She shuddered as she recalled a time when she was visiting with relatives in Wales, and her beastly cousin had shoved her into the root cellar and barricaded the door to keep her inside. She remembered screaming until she was hoarse before finally collapsing into a heap in the tiny space. A rat crawling across her leg roused her again, and she beat upon the door and screamed even louder until, finally, one of the servants heard the noise and released her. It was the last time they visited those particular relatives. That memory made her more determined to do what she needed to keep these pirates from doing her harm. It would serve no purpose to fight them; they would only hurt her more in retaliation.

"I promise not to try to hurt any of you, only let me have my hands." There was no response from without, and she resumed her struggle against her bonds until at last she could feel what she assumed was blood trickling down her wrists. She slumped into the chair, resigned for the moment to her fate. Before finally succumbing to the need to sleep, she whispered, "Colleen ... I know you can find me. I'll try to be strong, as I know you would be. Do not give up on me, nor will I give up on you."

It was the urgency of her need to relieve her bladder that wakened Abby. With a groan, she sat up as straight as she could in her chair to lessen the ache in her back, but the pressure on her bladder became worse as she did so. Her eyes were accustomed to the gloomy dark, and she directed her voice toward the stairs leading out of her cramped cell. "Please, someone help me. I have need of..." Embarrassment at having to state the reason for her distress caused her to cut off her words. But within a few minutes, she knew she must either get the attention of one of the pirates or suffer the indignity of soiling herself, and she raised her voice yet again. "Bring me a chamber pot, I beg of you. Someone..." At the sound of the hatch door opening, she grew quiet, hoping the one without was not one of the "less gentle" ones to whom the lady pirate had alluded.

"Quiet, lass. If you rouse old Jack, there'll be hell to pay. He's already dreaming of how to spend the prize your father will give for your safe return."

Abby could not make out the face of the sailor in the doorway, but the voice was familiar. It was the one from town, the one who said he was from the *Betsy Ann*. And she was not altogether sure he was truly a male. "I'll be quiet, but I need to ... relieve..."

"Shh, I heard you." Abby could hear the sailor approaching, and within a moment, the rope that bound her hands was free. Another few twists of the rope and her legs were no longer tight against the chair.

"Oh, thank you. Will you please take me to a washroom where I might—"

Mary's laughter stopped her short. "A washroom is it you want? Well, sorry to disappoint you, lass, but the best we can do is a slop bucket. Trust that won't hurt your tender bum too badly."

"Anything, please. And some privacy for decency's sake, I beg you. And some light to see by would be most welcome, if it is not too much to ask."

"Here's the bucket," Mary said, thrusting her own bucket into Abby's hand. She'd been on her way back to her bunk after dumping it overboard when she heard the captive calling out. "I'll fetch a candle if you can hold on for just a few moments, but woe upon you if you do any funny business with it, or it'll mean both our heads."

"I promise I will make no effort to harm or to escape. Just hurry, please."

Mary hurried up the steps and returned a few minutes later with a lit lantern and a stub of candle. She lit the candle and placed it on a bag of flour. "I'll be just outside the door, so give a little shout when you're decent, and I'll come back for the pot." She climbed the steps and dropped the door shut softly.

Mary was nodding off against the wall of the hold when she heard the captive's voice softly call out. Despite the woman's promise to behave, Mary nonetheless stood well back from the entrance of the hold as she opened the door. She need not have feared, for the prisoner was as far from the door as she could get in the confined space, and her hands were clearly empty of any weapons. "I'm coming down, lass. Kindly keep your hands where I can see them, as I would hate to have to hurt such a beautiful girl as yourself."

"I promised I would not attempt to harm you, sir, and I'm a woman of my word." Her tone of voice was offended and angry. Clearly, she was not used to having her word doubted.

"My lady, forgive me. I forgot you're not the type of woman in whose company I normally find myself. I shall not forget again." Mary picked up the slop bucket and headed for the stairs but stopped and once again turned toward the captive. "I shall return shortly with something for you to eat. Until then, I hope you can be reasonably comfortable in such cramped quarters."

"Thank you for your kindness, sir. Might I ask your name and whether it would be appropriate for me to address you by the same?"

"They call me Mark Read, my lady, and I would be honored to have you call me that."

"And I am Abigail Hume, Mr. Read. Abby is what my parents and friends call me, and I would allow you to use that name, as well, only I need for you to answer a question for me first. In town, you told me you had arrived aboard the *Betsy Ann*." Mary nodded, and Abby continued. "Was the name plucked from your imagination or have you actually encountered that vessel on your journeys?"

"Part of what I told you was true. The *Betsy Ann* was birthed in Nassau port as I disembarked. It appeared she might have just arrived as they were tying up as I walked by. I could not very well tell you I was from the *William* as that is a fairly well-known pirate ship. I simply chose the name of a vessel I knew to be on your shores at the time."

Abby's heart lurched in her chest at the thought she'd missed Colleen by only the slimmest of margins. Had she waited for a few hours to undertake her chores in town, she may have been home when Colleen came to call. Certainly, she would not now be held captive in the foul-smelling hold of a pirate ship. "I see. Well, it's my miserable luck you chose that name, for I do have a friend on board who comes to call when they're in port. Had you said the *Queen Anne's Revenge* or something instead, I would certainly not have accompanied you."

Mary laughed. "I trust you would not since that is another vessel full of pirates. Miss Hume, you may not believe me, but I truly hope your father will simply pay the ransom as required so we may set you free unharmed. I don't wish to cause you pain, even by not being able to prevent my shipmates from doing so. I hope your friend will not attempt a rescue, for I have indeed seen the *Betsy Ann*, and I can assure you the *William* can out-gun and out-man her, and only misfortune will be the result of such folly. Now if you'll excuse me, I'll see what victuals I can scare up for you."

As the hatch door gently closed behind Mary, Abby whispered, "The misfortune shall be yours, Mr. Read." She sat in the chair, grateful that Read had not bound her hands and feet again and had left the candle so she was not completely in the dark.

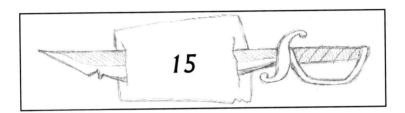

15

The *Betsy Ann* called at the port of Nassau a week earlier than the promised five months. As soon as the ship was tied, Colleen raised the blue scarf and made her way to the governor's house, but on this occasion, the governor and his family were not at home. She composed a brief letter for Abby and left it with a servant, who would share nothing about the whereabouts of the family, nor their intended return. Without knowing whether Abby was even on the island, there was no way for Colleen to know if she would be able to see her before the *Betsy Ann* departed three days hence. With a heavy heart, Colleen made her way back to the ship.

Charles looked up from his ledger at the sound of footsteps plodding by his door. Colleen was usually at her happiest those times when they called at Nassau, and he observed her leaving with a spring in her step not an hour before. This dispirited creature bore no resemblance to his lovely daughter. Rising from his chair, he caught up with her as she was about to enter her quarters. "Colleen, stop a moment, won't you, for a word with your old father?" The face she turned upon him was drawn, and her eyes showed none of their normal luster. "Pray, come into my quarters and tell me what has you so stricken."

"It's ... nothing, Father." Tears fairly brimmed in her eyes, but she resolutely forbade them to fall.

"Oh, lass, I've seen 'nothing,' and such is not the look upon your face. I hope you know you can speak freely to me about anything. You're my world, Col, and I wish only for your happiness." He turned his chair to face the door and held out his hand for Colleen to take.

His outstretched hand was her undoing. With a sob, she took it and allowed him to draw her onto his lap. She buried her face in his neck seeking the comfort his familiar scent brought to her in her youth. But there was no consoling her this time; she knew it could be as much as half a year before she might see Abby again, and the pain was as deep as if an iron band was clamped around her heart.

Charles was alarmed at her condition. Even upon his return home to find his wife and sons dead, Colleen did not appear as distressed as this. Stroking her hair, he whispered softly, "I can't bear to see you so grief-stricken, Col. Please, tell me what has you so saddened and if your old father can do anything at all to help."

Colleen simply hugged him more tightly and continued to sob. He held her and hummed a lively melody, which normally brought a smile to her face, and after a few minutes, the sobs diminished and finally stopped. She sat up on his lap and brushed the tears away from her cheeks, embarrassed to have shown such weakness in front of him. "Forgive me for behaving like a child, Father." She rose from his lap and turned to leave. "I shall let you get back to your work."

Charles caught her hand once again before she was out of reach. "Please stay and talk to me. Perhaps I can help, or at the very least make you less sad." He pulled his footstool over near his desk and motioned for her to sit.

With a sigh, Colleen sat, her long legs stretched out before her. "I'm not sure how to talk to you about this, Father. It's ... I mean, bloody hell, I find I can't speak about ... such things with you."

Charles seemed to understand. "Would this be something you

would normally have discussed with your mother?" At Colleen's nod, he continued. "You were old enough to have discussed the womanly issues with her, I know. I suspect now it's more an issue of the heart. Is this the case, my dear?"

"Yes, Father. I have fallen in love. I never expected to ... meet someone who could make me feel this way. I am at once giddy as a schoolgirl and serious as a broken arm. My mood is light when we are together and dark the farther away we are from each other. This ... person lives here, in Nassau. I find I'm only truly alive when I'm here." Colleen dropped her head to her chest, unable to meet her father's eyes.

Charles was taken aback. The fact that Colleen referred to her beloved as a person, and not as a man, was a telling thing. The more he thought about it, however, the more sense it made. Colleen had lived for many years in the company of nothing but men, and none appeared to have caught her fancy at all. Charles had long before given up trying to match his beautiful daughter with eligible bachelors since she refused to even meet them. He knew a few men who preferred the company of their own gender; there were one or two aboard ship at any given time. This did not trouble Charles, so long as they accomplished their duties as required and made no overtures toward those others of his crew who were not like-minded. He never thought there might be women who also kept to their own kind, but he suspected such was the case with Colleen. Choosing his words carefully, he said, "And does she return your love, Colleen?"

Colleen's head snapped up, her mouth open in an O shape. Words deserted her for the moment, and she could only nod.

"I confess it did not occur to me until now to credit your lack of interest in men to an attraction to the fairer sex. However, as I look back, it seems as clear as anything to me. Men were friends and comrades to you, never more than that."

"I ... yes, you are exactly right. I never found a man who appealed to me ... as it seemed he should. Oh, but my heart sings when she is in my presence. I was not certain how you might receive this news, or I would have told you before. I could not bear to hurt you, nor risk the loss of your affection. You've been my world, Father. I should hate to be a disappointment to you."

"Oh, Col, you are anything but a disappointment. You have been both son and daughter to me, and I tried to give you the support a mother might have. And I meant it when I said your happiness is all I desire. If this woman gives you the love you deserve, then I am happy for you."

Colleen jumped up from her stool and wrapped her arms around her father's neck, raining kisses upon his cheeks. Her eyes sparkled, and her mouth turned up in a smile. "You have lightened my heart, Father. I was fairly certain you would not shun me when I told you the truth, but even the slim chance you might made me hold my tongue. And you know I've always spoken my mind with you. It hurt me to hold this inside when I have confided my feelings to you in the past. What did I do to deserve such a kind and loving father as yourself?"

"Naught but be yourself, lass. I would have you no other way. Now tell me when I might expect to meet this lady who has captured your affections."

Colleen's eyes lost their spark, and with a sigh she said, "I wish I could say. She is not at home, and I have no idea when she might be, which accounts for my sour mood. I know you wish to set sail three days hence, and I don't know if she will return before then."

"Well then, let us see what we can do to sweeten your mood. We shall stay in port for two additional days or longer, if absolutely necessary. We are a bit ahead of schedule, so I'm sure a small delay will not be a problem. How is—"

Colleen launched herself into his arms again and hugged him with all her might, causing him to gasp. She loosened her hold but continued to hug him because it had been such a long time since she last did so, and it was comforting to feel him close to her. "Father, you make me so happy I could sing." And she did just that, launching into "The Mariner's Wife," which became her favorite song the moment she heard Abby singing it. Her father joined in, and at the end of the song, he clapped his daughter on the shoulder.

"These journal entries can wait," he said, slamming the

book shut. "Let's take ourselves off this old tub for a while and get some food that's not been sitting in the hold for weeks, eh? Perhaps you would even share a pint or two with your old dad. And afterward, we can make a few discreet inquiries about when you might expect to find your friend at home."

"Splendid, Dad!"

Colleen had not called him dad since she was five or six, but it seemed the right thing to say when a smile wreathed her father's face.

Charles took his three-cornered hat off the peg by the door and settled it on his head. He hooked his arm through hers as they made their way across the deck and down the gangplank, certain in the knowledge that the most beautiful woman in the world walked by his side.

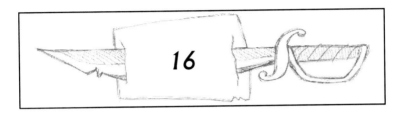

16

Colleen seldom touched liquor; the rum she and Abby shared while holed up in a cave professing their love for each other was the last she took, other than the small quantity normally mixed in the drinking water on board ship. The two glasses of wine she drank at dinner gave her a pleasant glow, and as she and her father walked from the inn to the tavern, they chatted about Abby. Colleen withheld her lover's name from him until such time as she could talk with Abby and make certain she would not have a problem with her divulging her feelings to her father.

When they entered the tavern, it was plain to see that something very out of the ordinary had occurred. The noise level was so loud she could not make out exactly what was going on, but the words governor, daughter, and Calico Jack occasionally piercing through the din made her flesh crawl. She pushed her way past several of the sailors who were grouped around a well-dressed man and woman. The man was pacing and gesturing with his cane, and the woman was sitting in a chair moaning and crying.

"I tell you, something must be done now!" the man bellowed, and the noise level dropped when he rapped his ivory-handled cane on the tabletop several times. "That blackguard must not be allowed to leave these waters with my daughter!"

Charles and five other privateers met with the governor two years earlier to discuss problems arising from the Spaniard claims to several of the local islands, and he recognized the governor at once. He immediately made his way to where the half-crazed man stood, attempting to comfort his hysterical wife. "Lord Hume, you may not remember me, but we met some years ago. I am Charles Edwards Esquire, captain of the *Betsy Ann*. My ship and all her crew are at your disposal. What is it that distresses you and your wife so?"

"Have you not been listening, man? That pirate ... that ... Jack Rackham has kidnapped my daughter. He said he would return her to me unharmed on Saturday a week if I bring to him a thousand pounds. But I fear those animals on board that cursed vessel will not honor the promise he made. I fear for her ... health, her womanhood. If they hurt her, by Christ..." His bravado faded away and he collapsed into a chair beside his wife.

Colleen's face lost all color, and she clutched the back of a chair to keep herself from collapsing, as well. The *Betsy Ann* was fortunate to have avoided any direct conflict with Jack Rackham, but Colleen knew there was very little the notorious pirate could do to stop his men if they took it upon themselves to have their way with Abby. Thinking about what could befall her lover, she became angry. Her anger effectively shored up her resolve to rescue Abby.

"And how is it you are to deliver this ransom to him and recover your daughter?" she asked. The man looked up at the tall blue-eyed woman, whose cheeks blazed with anger, then to the captain who stood beside her. Charles nodded to let him know Colleen was with him.

"I am to bring it to a pub in Port Royal at noon on Saturday. He says he will deliver my daughter when he has verified the count." Colleen gritted her teeth. She knew it was not likely the man would return Abby, whether the count was true or not. In fact, Abby might already be lying on the bottom of the ocean. No, she could not afford to think like that. It would only slow her down, and speed was of the essence now.

"Father, we must pursue him before he is so far away we can't hope to catch him. Her peril increases every moment she's on board that ship."

"There will be a substantial reward in this for you if you bring her safely back to me," Lord Hume said, taking heart from the knowledge that Captain Edwards and his crew would go after the man. "But if you fail, I must be prepared in Port Royal to pay the ransom, in case..." He could not finish the thought.

Charles gave the governor what he hoped was a reassuring pat on the arm and said, "Too right. You must book passage on the next ship that will take you there. If God is with us, we will hand her to you before you are forced to pay the ransom."

"I care nothing about the ransom. Please, just bring my child back to us." His voice cracked, and once again, the tears spilled from his eyes.

Charles and Colleen made haste in returning to the *Betsy Ann* where the crew was directed to quickly unload the cargo they carried to lighten the weight of the ship and give her more speed. Before the sunset, they were en route to Port Royal, in the hope of intercepting the *William* with their faster ship.

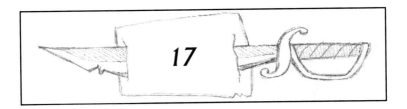

Time crawled by with the speed of a snail as Abby sat in the confines of the dank foul-smelling hold with only the occasional visits from Anne with food, or Read, on whose lot fell the care of Abby's personal needs. It seemed Jack Rackham intended to carry through with his promise to leave her unharmed, as no other sailor approached her door.

Late in the afternoon of the second day, when Read showed up with a meager repast, Abby clutched his sleeve. "Mr. Read, please allow me to go topside for a while to get some fresh air and light. I can scarcely breathe in this stifling heat and am nearly mad with inactivity and darkness. Please, sir, I beg you. I'll give you no reason to regret your kindness."

Since their first encounter on board ship, both had formed something of a respect for each other, and Read allowed Abby to remain untied while within her cell. It was quite a different matter, however, to bring her up on deck where the other sailors might get their hands on her. Read could not defend her charge against most of the brutes on board.

"I'll take you out for a bit, Miss Hume, but I can't do so without securing you to me in the event of rough seas. Kindly hold out your hands." Abby did as requested, and Read reached out to tie her wrists, but upon noticing the angry red welts from when she was captured, thought better of it and secured the rope around her waist instead. The free end of the rope Read looped around her belt with enough space between them so they could walk side by side without touching. Climbing the stairs of the hold was a challenge, but Read surmounted it by simply picking Abby up and carrying her. The surprised look on Abby's face when Read set her on the deck was enough to make Read laugh out loud. "I'm sorry if I was too forward, Miss Hume, but it seemed the only way to get you out of the hold safely."

Abby's cheeks flamed a bright red, but she finally smiled at Read, whose laugh had been infectious. "I'm constantly surprised at you, Mr. Read. First you trick me and capture me, and now you treat me with the familiarity of an old friend. Tell me, do you treat all your prisoners in this fashion?"

"Ah, no. But then I've never been charged with taking care of a captive as lovely as you. And truly, I might not have nicked you at all but for Anne, who indicated I should. She's the captain's ... consort, I suppose you could say. If she wishes for something to be done, then done it is."

"I see." From the brief interactions she had witnessed between Anne and Read, Abby believed the two were involved, so it came as something of a surprise to learn the captain was enjoying Anne's favors. With a shrug, she dismissed the thought as they arrived on deck, and the sight of the sun painting brilliant colors across the horizon made Abby forget about Read and Anne and whatever their relationship might be. She made her way to the railing where she leaned over and pulled the tangy salt smell into her lungs, wishing she had her paints and canvas with her to capture the glorious panorama of the vanishing day. "Oh, Mr. Read, how fortunate you are to be able to look upon this beauty every day. I only hope I will have my freedom soon to take in this miracle, as well."

"I wish the same for you, Miss Hume. Day after tomorrow this time, we should be in Port Royal, and one day hence you will be free." She did not add the freedom would be contingent upon Abby's father paying the ransom. She could not bear dwelling on what Jack Rackham might do if the governor failed to deliver the gold.

"Well, if it ain't her highness herself out taking the air." Abby turned abruptly to look upon the face of a sailor who had approached stealthily and grasped her arm. Because of the tether attaching them, Read was jerked to Abby's side, nearly knocking her over the rail. She quickly righted her charge and turned to glare at the sailor who had startled them both.

"Leave off, Dobbs. Jack says you lot are to keep your hands off Miss Hume."

Dobbs snorted with disdain. He was quite a bit taller than Read and outweighed him by at least three stone. "And who is it that's gonna stop me, eh? I can tie you in knots and toss you to the sharks and nobody can—"

"This knife says I can," Anne purred in his ear. None of them had noticed the fiery Irish woman as she crept up behind Dobbs and placed the tip of her knife just under his ribs. "We'll have yer heart for supper if you don't back off the lady, bucko. And don't think I won't be tellin' Jack about what you tried to do."

Dobbs drew in his breath to try to remove his flesh from the bite of the knife, but Anne only pushed it higher, nicking him hard enough to draw blood. "Aw, Anne, I was only havin' a bit of fun. I wasn't going to hurt the lady none." He raised his hands in the air to show he held no weapons, and Anne withdrew the knife, wiping the blood it held on his shirt. He let out a breath and backed away from the trio, not turning his back until he was well out of reach.

"Stupid sod," Anne muttered, sliding her knife back into its sheath.

"I could've handled him," Read said under her breath, but the words were not lost on Anne, who turned to glare at her.

"And just how were you plannin' on doing that, with her ladyship all tied up to you like an anchor? The two of you were about to be feedin' the fish. And why in nine kinds of hell did you bring her up on deck to get these brutes stirred up, anyway? Jack trusted us to take care of the prize. Am I going to have to be tellin' him yer not up to the task?" Her cheeks flamed, and she fisted her hands on her hips. In truth, she was more than just a little bit jealous of the governor's daughter. Abby was far prettier than herself, and her words and manner were soft and appealing. She could tell by the way Read looked at Abby that she was attracted to her. If there were another sailor on board to be trusted, Anne might have suggested Jack assign someone else to watch after the prize, but she feared it might arouse his suspicion.

Abby insinuated herself between the two of them. "Please don't blame him for this. I all but insisted he bring me on deck, and he was merely trying to make me more comfortable. And I don't think the sailor meant to harm me."

"Ah, don't be too sure, yer ladyship. These blokes will rape you as soon as look at you. The only thing they understand is violence. So if you want to come on deck again ... and I'm not saying you will be allowed, mind ... then you need to make sure Read and meself are there to watch out for you. Clear?"

"Yes, clear. Thank you."

"We're about to lose the light, so we better get you below deck while we can still see." Anne took Abby's elbow, and Read took the other arm, and together they made their way to the hold. Read untied the rope from around Abby's waist.

"Thank you, Mr. Read. I'm sorry if I was the cause of trouble for you."

"No trouble, Miss Hume. No trouble at all." The sound of Anne's "hmph" as she walked away belied the statement, but Read pretended not to hear it. "I shall return shortly with some supper for you and another candle. I trust you will be all right until then."

"I have seen the sunset, Mr. Read. That will sustain me until the candle illuminates my cell." She touched Read's cheek lightly with her fingers, noting the absolute absence of whiskers. "And thank you again for your kindness."

Abby's candle had burned out long enough before that it was now completely cold, so she had no idea whether it was day or night. Read was kind enough to leave her with a bucket of her own so she no longer had to call out for help when she needed to relieve her bladder. She took care of that chore and placed the bucket under the stairs where she would not inadvertently knock it over. Her back was stiff from lying so long on the pallet, so she paced from one end to the other of the small area. Her eyes were accustomed enough to the dim light that she could make out shapes and avoid colliding with them as she walked.

As she turned to make yet another circuit of her cell, her shoulder brushed against a small wooden box balanced on top of a larger stack of boxes. It went tumbling to the floor, spilling its contents in a heap at her feet. She bent to retrieve the items, fearing that Anne or Read might come in and accuse her of trying to steal something and punish her. There was not enough light to truly see what she held, but from the feel of it, one item was a leather belt or harness of some sort. The other was shaped rather like a small club, but it appeared to be covered in leather. She brought it closer to her face to try to get a better idea of what it was and could not help but notice it bore the lingering scent of a woman's private part upon it. "What's this then?" The leather belt had a hole in it that seemed large enough to accommodate the club, which had a round piece of leather sewn onto one end. Curiosity drove her to see if it would indeed fit, and it did; the round piece at the end held it firmly in place. "Well, well," she chuckled. "Somebody seems to be playing a part. I wonder if Mr. Read continues her masquerade even in bed, and if so, there is no other female on board to play with except Anne. Do I dare tell her what I have learned?"

The sound of the lock being removed from the door of the hold pulled her from her ruminations, and she quickly returned the items to the box and placed it where it had been. She turned and saw sunlight spilling through the door, and she shielded her eyes from the brightness. A moment later, Read clambered through the door and down the stairs, a lit candle in one hand and a burlap sack in the other.

"Morning, your grace," she said cheerfully. "Thought your candle might have been gone by now." She handed the candle to Abby, who placed it in the pool of wax left by the old one.

"Thank you, Mr. Read. Now I can resume my reading of

Chaucer while I drink my tea." She laughed and dropped a curtsy. Mary bowed in return, then held out the burlap sack.

"Here's a bit of cheese and bread to go with your tea, Princess." She winked at the use of the title, given to Abby by none other than Jack Rackham. It had come to be a joke between the two of them. "Anne is ah … indisposed this morning and asked me to bring this to you." She did not add that Anne was not successful in causing her baby to miscarry, and Jack had knocked her around, bruising a few ribs, when she was finally forced to tell him about the pregnancy. Mary was glad her disguise allowed her to avoid the possibility of pregnancy.

Abby's stomach growled at the mere mention of food. It felt like months she'd been confined to this hold, with nothing more to eat than porridge or stale bread and cheese and nothing to drink but water laced with rum. But in fact, it had been only three days since she was taken captive. And despite the likely distasteful offering, her hunger drove her to reach out and accept the sack. "I'm grateful to you for bringing this to me. I'm sure you have better things to do." Abby sat down on a box and withdrew a small chunk of cheese from the sack. She scraped off a bit of mold with her fingernail before taking a bite. The bread was so hard she couldn't eat it without dunking it in water, which did nothing to improve the taste of either. When Read did not immediately withdraw, Abby put the food down beside her water goblet and gestured for her to sit on a nearby box. "I'm tired of my own voice, Mr. Read. It would please me if you could keep me company while I eat."

"I don't mind taking a load off for a few minutes, Princess. A few of the lads are down with the grippe, so I've more than a bit of work to do." She dropped down beside Abby and smiled at her. The more time she spent with Abby, the more she liked the feisty woman. More than once, she wished they'd met under different circumstances.

"Ah, you mean working to stay away from them so you don't catch it, I'll warrant."

"Well, yes, mostly. And Jack is in a foul temper, so I'm trying to stay out of his path. He's a mean one when he's riled."

Abby had only spoken to the pirate captain once since her capture, but it was enough to let her know he was no gentleman, if in fact such a person existed among his kind. "You're welcome to remain here as long as you like. I don't get many visitors, and I grow weary of the isolation." She laughed. "It's funny; at home I might spend days with no other company but Susan, and yet I do not feel lonely. Here I am hungry for the sound of another voice, the image of a friendly face. And I find you to be friendly, Mr. Read. If I didn't know you were a pirate, I might have taken you for a ... gentleman. You have a softness about you." When Mary looked up with something akin to fear on her face, Abby quickly continued, "And I find that a most endearing quality. In fact, I find myself most drawn to people like you. Soft, yet strong, capable of even the most daunting tasks and at the same time gentle and considerate. Do you understand my meaning, Mr. Read?"

The emphasis on "mister" was undeniable. Mary looked into Abby's sea green eyes and saw only kindness and acceptance. "I couldn't be a gentleman, even if I was not a pirate. But I suppose you know that." Abby smiled and nodded for Mary to continue. "When me father died, the only way his family would continue to support Mother was if she had a male heir. She'd given birth to a boy who died in infancy. When I came along, she let them think I was he. She dressed me up as a boy from the time I was small and called me Mark from then on. I was christened Mary, but Mary I would not be again for many years. Mother died when I was around fifteen. After that, I joined the army to have a place to sleep and food to eat. I met a man while I was in the army. I could tell he fancied me, and I thought he knew I was a woman. We married when he was discharged from the service, but we never shared a great love. I found out he actually thought I was a man when he fell in love with me, and in truth, I married him for the farm his family left him." She shrugged as if to say times were hard, and you did what you had to do to survive. "We lived together almost as brother and sister for nearly ten years until he died. I had neither the skill nor the money to run the farm on my own, and when I could not pay the taxes, his cousins were quick to lay claim to the farm, and I was out in the cold again with no place to go. I put on men's clothes and joined the Royal Navy. Not two years later, I was on board the *William* when she was taken by Calico Jack, and I was forced into piracy to avoid having me throat cut. I guess I'm a pirate now, right enough. But if I'd known you before I saw you in the apothecary shop, I never would have taken you, and that's the truth. You don't deserve whatever fate waits for you if your father is not there by the appointed time to deliver the gold."

"Och, he'll be there, Mary, I've no doubt."

Hearing her name trip so easily off Abby's tongue gave Mary a thrill that ran up her body, leaving goose flesh in its wake. "Is there someone waiting for you, Abby? I don't mean your father and mother…"

"Yes, there is, or perhaps she's not waiting, but already in pursuit of this vessel. If she knew I was here, nothing would stop her from rescuing me, I know." She held her head high and looked Mary directly in the eye.

"Lucky Colleen from the *Betsy Ann*, is it?" When Abby nodded, Mary shook her head sadly. "I might have known. I finally meet a proper girl, one who truly fancies other girls instead of dabbling at it, and she's in love with a bloody sailor."

Abby laughed and kissed Mary lightly on the cheek, causing her to blush profusely. "Don't give up, Mary. There's somebody out there for each of us, I believe. But you may have a hard time finding her if you stay on this cursed ship."

"I'm as cursed as the ship, Abby. And there's no way off but to a watery grave."

"Not if I can do anything to help," Abby said.

The determined look on her face almost made Mary believe her.

"Oh, and, Mary, I found something interesting in the hold. It was about so long," she held her fingers about six inches apart, "and covered in leather. Any idea what it might be? And more importantly, where I might find such an item?"

Mary burst out laughing. "I just might be able to help with that, Princess."

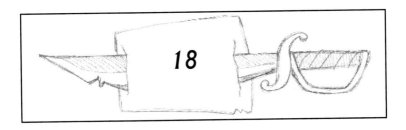

18

Just after sunset three days out from port, the lookout in the crow's nest of the *Betsy Ann* spotted the flag of the *William*. "Pirate ship to starboard!"

Charles ordered the ship brought to bear on the larger vessel, maintaining a distance that would put them out of reach of her cannons in the event they were seen. He hoped the fading light would give them the element of surprise, and he and four well-armed crewmen could take the jolly boat and catch them by surprise.

Alas, Calico Jack himself stood at the railing relieving his bladder and saw the little boat approaching. He called for a crewman to bring him a musket, and when the jolly boat was within range, he fired at the man in the red jacket, figuring he was the highest-ranking person aboard the ship pursuing them. "Hah!" he crowed when he heard the unmistakable cry of someone who'd been shot. "There's more o' those for any man who tries to board the *William*," he called loudly enough for them to hear.

The flash from the muzzle followed immediately by the echoing report of the musket told Colleen that her father's attempt to approach the pirate ship and board her unawares was not successful.

"They're firing on him, Col," Gordon called from the crow's nest, but his words were a confirmation of what her own eyes and ears already told her. "Someone's been hit, I think! The jolly boat is turning around." Despite the darkness, from his vantage point high up on the mainmast, and with his spy glass, he knew better than Colleen what was going on.

"Get a rope ladder over the side," Colleen ordered the nearest sailor as she made a dash for the railing. He beat her there by only a few moments, and she was over the side and down to water level, watching for the returning jolly boat. She heard the oars slapping the water and the grunts of the sailors as they hauled away for all they were worth to reach the *Betsy Ann*.

"Ahoy, on deck! The captain's been shot!"

Colleen almost lost her grip on the rope when she heard those words, and her heart seized in her chest. She could not lose him; he was the only family she had left, and they depended upon each other more than either of them truly realized. She took a deep breath and reached down to take hold of the rope offered by the sailor and secure the small boat. "Is he—alive?" she asked, praying the answer would be yes and that he was merely wounded.

"He is, but he's in a bad way, Col. We need help to get him on board."

Colleen clambered back up the rope ladder and motioned for Pickles, the tallest and strongest man on board, to climb into the small boat. "Tie him onto your back, Pickles, and carry him up if you can. If he's too heavy, we'll try to relay him up the ladder."

"Nae worry, Col. I'll get him up here right enough, and none the worse than he is now. He'll be all right, lass." Draping a length of rope around his neck and under his arm, he scuttled over the edge with the agility of a dancer. For a large man, he was extremely graceful and gentle. Only a few minutes later, Pickles's head appeared once again above the railing, and two other sailors hurried to help him climb aboard.

Colleen gasped when she saw the condition her father was in. Captain Charles Edwards was unconscious, the wound to his chest an unbelievably large hole, and he had clearly lost a lot of blood. His face was ashen and clammy as they laid his body on the deck.

Tears welled in her eyes, and she turned toward the pirate ship now a mere speck in the distance. "Damn you, Jack Rackham! I'll send you to Davy Jones's locker for this." She dropped to her knees beside him, Mr. Henry on the other side.

"We 'ave to get 'im to a real doctor, lass," James said, laying his hand on her shoulder. "'E ain't got a hope if we don't do it soon."

Colleen knew she had no choice; her father's life would be forfeit if she did not make for shore immediately. Turning toward the pirate ship, she promised silently she would meet him herself in Port Royal, and nothing would stop her from taking Abby off that ship. "Turn her about, Mr. Henry. Make for Andros Island." Like Port Royal, at any given time, Andros Island had more than its share of pirates. Colleen hoped none of them would take a fancy to the *Betsy Ann*. She would fight if she had to, but could ill afford the delay in having her father seen to, then continuing her pursuit of the *William*.

"Lass, I've got ever'thing prepared ye asked for." Colleen heard Mr. Henry's voice as if from far away. She raised her head from her arms, which rested on the side of her father's bed. They were fortunate to put ashore within walking distance of a doctor and quickly roused him before transporting her father there on a litter. He was able to remove the bullet but was not holding out much hope for the captain's survival. He'd lost a lot of blood. The next few days would tell the tale.

"Thank you, Mr. Henry. We need to make ready then. Please ask Mr. Poppitt to come in here." Poppitt had been one of the sailors aboard the jolly boat with the captain, and he was sick with worry over his condition. Poppitt volunteered to keep vigil at her father's bedside and suggested the rest of the crew take shifts, as well, to relieve Colleen of the burden. She was grateful for the assistance, especially since she planned to be back at sea as soon as the wind was up.

Colleen took her father's hand in her own. The hand was still and pale, so unlike the man she knew that she very nearly looked down to make certain it was her father whose hand was cradled in her own. Tears fell as she beheld his ashen face, and she prayed she would once again see it lively and colorful. She whispered so that none other in the room might hear, "Father, my heart aches to see you thus, and I would do anything in my power to make you well again. But my skills do not include healing, so I must trust you to Dr. Pomerleau's care. God willing, you will be on the road to recovery when I return for you, and I pray the woman I love will be safe beside me. I love you, Dad." She kissed his cheek and brushed the hair from his eyes, and with a sigh, she rose from her chair and walked from the room.

Colleen grasped the luxurious black hair that cascaded down her back and pulled it over her shoulder. Without hesitation, she sawed off most of the length of it, leaving just enough to be gathered up by a leather strap and hang on her neck, which is how her father wore his hair. Satisfied with the look of her hair, she took a bolt of cloth used for making bandages and wound it tightly around her chest several times. She could not completely hide her breasts, but she hoped it would simply appear she had pronounced muscles in her chest. She stitched the cloth to keep it in place and donned her father's dress jacket and trousers. He was broader in the shoulder than she was, but their height and girth were nearly the same, so she hoped the small misfit in the shoulders would not be noticeable. She slid her feet into his knee-high boots and pulled them up. After walking around the cabin for a few minutes, she knew she could not wear those boots without some padding, so she removed them and put on several pairs of stockings. When she put them on again, she felt comfortable to walk about. She removed her father's French cocked hat from his closet and settled it on her head. And finally, she strapped his rapier about her waist, completing the look. At least until she had succeeded in freeing Abby, she would remain Captain Charles Edwards the second. She hoped her father would be able to resume his duties at some point in the future, so her thoughts only went as far as rescuing the woman she loved.

Mr. Henry lined up the twelve new crewmen he hired for this

voyage. Colleen was not certain her father's crew would obey her orders, and she certainly could not convince them she had suddenly become a man. Therefore it was necessary to find men who'd never before crewed for her father, and thus were not aware that his son Charles had perished in his youth. Colleen walked up and back in front of the men, assessing their strengths visually. She nodded; Mr. Henry had done an excellent job of selecting these men. She briefly assigned each man his duty and informed all of them they would be pushing hard and sailing through the nights if necessary until they reached Port Royal. She did not tell them what her mission there was, merely that it was of an urgent nature and must be completed with all speed. None of the men hesitated to comply with her wishes. To them, she was the capable captain of the *Betsy Ann*, and her orders were to be obeyed without question.

Colleen was lucky if she managed two or three hours of sleep a night for the next three days. She and Mr. Henry took turns at the helm, and the twelve crewmen likewise napped for brief periods before going back on duty. She drove them hard but had promised them a substantial reward at the end of the voyage, and they were more than willing to work.

For her part, if she was not on deck, she was planning what she would do when they arrived at Port Royal. She had no intention of going up against Calico Jack and his crew as her father had attempted. She planned to sneak aboard ship and remove Abby while the crew slept. And if she was lucky, she would destroy the *William* when she was through.

Colleen was in her father's cabin sewing together pouches that she then filled with gunpowder. She planned to use them to blow holes in Rackham's ship and reckoned she would need about ten altogether. She had six of them complete when exhaustion overtook her, and she dropped off to sleep, her head resting on the desk. A sharp rap on the door roused her from her doze, and when she jerked upright in her seat, she stabbed herself with a needle. Sucking her finger, she mumbled a curse before calling out, "Enter."

James slipped into the room, a smile on his face. "We 'ave

done it, lass. Port Royal is in sight, and that blackguard's ship's sittin' there, pretty as ye please. And one day to spare before the ransom must be paid."

"Excellent news, Mr. Henry! Come, we must prepare for docking." They went topside, where Colleen trained her looking glass in the direction indicated by the man in the crow's nest. She saw the sloop flying Jack Rackham's standard—the skull with crossed swords. "I've as good as got you, you bastard. And I'll have your guts for garters if you've harmed a hair on Abby's head." She directed the crew to put ashore at a private dock some distance from where the pirate ship was moored. She feared Calico Jack would recognize the ship from their previous encounter and didn't want the pirate to know they were so close.

As soon as they were tied up, Colleen gave the crew leave to go ashore, saying they would be departing on Sunday latest. If she were able to complete her mission earlier, she would leave word at the local inn for them. Exhausted from pushing so hard for the past three days, the men were eager for the rest, and she did not expect to see anything of them until time to depart again. And that was just fine for her plan. When she and James were alone on board, she changed once again into her own clothes but left her breasts bound. To change her appearance so her crew would not recognize her, should they happen to be in the same establishment as herself, she used her father's bootblack and brush to create the illusion of beard stubble. She also covered one eye with a patch and pulled her hat down low to further camouflage her face. When she went ashore, she would appear to be a sailor on leave, and if she were lucky, she would find out what was going on aboard the *William.*

Colleen spent most of the day in the Hog's Breath Tavern with a half-empty mug of ale in front of her. When a new bunch of men would come in, she'd study their clothing, trying to determine if they were part of the pirate's crew, but as evening was falling, she was beginning to think her day had been a waste. It was at that moment she recognized the black and red colors of the pirate's crew. Pretending to be completely drunk, she raised her mug to the nearest of Calico Jack's crew and slurred, "Ahoy, mate," then immediately dropped her head to the bar as if she were passed out.

The sailor laughed and elbowed her in the ribs, nearly unseating her. "Out of the way, ye stupid sod. We 'ave some serious drinkin' to do before we 'ave to load some bleedin' cargo."

Pretending the elbow to the ribs had roused her, she mumbled, "Sorry, mate," and moved over to allow room for the men to crowd in at the bar. But she remained close enough to listen to the conversation. And she studied the men, assessing which of them would suit her purposes for the rest of her plan. It was not easy, considering she had to keep her eyes closed most of the time, but she did finally pick out a stubble-faced younger man, whose build was most like her own. When she finally knew as much as she needed to know about their plans for the evening, she lurched away from the bar and staggered across the room and out into the early evening. As soon as she was away from them, she stood upright and ran to find Mr. Henry, who had been performing a similar act at another tavern in the seaport town. She sent him back to the Hog's Breath to keep watch on the sailors while she went back to the ship to prepare for the next part of her plan.

Colleen waited near the corner of the warehouse where the pirate crew would soon be arriving to collect their cargo. She watched them pass by her hiding place until the young man she'd selected to replace approached, and she stumbled into him, crying out, "Beg pardon, sir. Please, I beg a boon of thee. I 'ave lost me three shillings 'ere on me way to buy some bread to feed me wee ones. Me wife'll kill me if I come 'ome without it, but 'tis practically blind I am, and I can't find 'em. Would you be so kind as to 'elp me search?"

The young man nodded and bent over to see if he could find the coins, and Colleen hit him sharply on the back of the head. She caught him before he could hit the ground and dragged him to a place she'd scouted in advance. She quickly removed his clothes and afterward laid him on his stomach with his hands and feet bound together over his back. To ensure he didn't call out to his mates, she stuffed a cloth in his mouth and secured it behind his head. She pulled his trousers and shirt on over her own and clamped his hat on her head. Returning to her hiding place by the entrance to the warehouse, she waited for the crew to begin marching out, each one carrying a wooden box. Collecting her box of gunpowder bundles from where they were hidden, she fell in line behind the last man. As the men boarded the ship, she held the crate so it partially blocked her face, and no one gave her a second look. Knowing the men would by now have eaten their evening meal, she made her way to the galley, where she hid behind sacks of flour and salt and waited for the ship to quiet down.

Several hours later, she crept from her hiding place, bringing her wooden box along. She made her way past the crew's quarters to a door leading to the hold that had a lock on the outside. This must certainly be where Abby was being held. She withdrew two iron picks from her boot and inserted them into the lock. After several minutes of patiently working at it, she heard the soft click of the lock releasing. With a smile, she removed the lock, but before she opened the door, she hung it in such a way that it would appear to be engaged if someone simply glanced in that direction. Picking up her box, she quietly opened the door and made her way down the steps into the hold.

It was completely dark inside the cramped space, so she stood for several minutes allowing her eyes to become accustomed to the dark. She heard the even sounds of someone breathing in sleep and turned toward the sound. There was no question she'd found what she sought; even in the gloom, she could make out the blond curls that tumbled over the pillow on the pallet. She crept closer and got down on her knees beside the sleeping woman. Knowing that Abby would likely cry out before she knew who was there, she placed her hand over her mouth, and sure enough, Abby opened her mouth as if to scream before she heard a familiar voice saying, "Abby, shhh, please, don't make a sound. I've come to rescue you." The tension left Abby's body, and as soon as it did, Colleen removed her hand. Abby sat up on her pallet, throwing her arms around Colleen's neck and pulling her close.

"Thank God! I knew if anybody could, you would find a way to save me from these brutes."

"We're not out of here yet, Abby. Put these clothes on." She handed her some clothing belonging to the cabin boy aboard the *Betsy Ann*, which she reckoned would fit. She could not hope to get her off the ship in all her finery if there was a guard on deck, as she would expect to find on such a ship. She turned her back as Abby shucked off the nightgown Anne had given her to wear and pulled on the short pants and shirt Colleen had provided.

"Here are some shoes and stockings, as well. I suspect they'll not fit very well, but you need not wear them for long," Colleen whispered. When Abby held the shoes and stockings at arm's length, Colleen quickly added, "Sorry about the aroma, but they were the best I could find on board."

Abby drew the stockings over her own, which were none too clean either after a week in the hold, but she knew she didn't have the luxury of choice here. She pushed her long hair up into the cap Colleen handed her to finish off the disguise. She stood up to get the feel of the shoes, and each step she took resounded loudly against the boards.

"Step softly, love, or you'll rouse every lout on this tub."

"Oh, sorry." She took a few more steps and the sound was considerably less. "Do I look like a sailor, Col? I feel like a child playing dress-up in her father's trunk of old clothes. You think I will not arouse their suspicion?"

"It should work if they don't look too closely. I'll pretend to be a drunken sailor needing assistance, and you will appear to be helping me walk. That way, we can hope your breasts don't give away your gender, if they are pressed up against the side of my body." Even as she said those words, her own body shivered at the thought of those breasts pressed up against her. Abby nodded her agreement and took hold of Colleen's hand. She pressed her lips against her protector's softly.

"For luck," she said with a smile. Colleen kissed her back, just a bit harder.

"For luck," she agreed. She collected the wooden box containing the rest of the things she would need and led Abby up the steps.

They made no noise as they approached the prow of the ship,

and Colleen scanned the deck for the guard. Wordlessly, she tapped Abby on the shoulder and pointed to starboard. The guard was leaning against the railing, his eyes on a sailor he had seen on the pier. It was James Henry, Colleen hoped. He was to make himself seen but not make any moves toward the vessel, in the hope that the guard would be too preoccupied with him to notice Colleen and Abby until it was too late. Colleen stashed her wooden box behind a coil of rope, draped her arm over Abby's shoulder, and gestured for Abby to wrap her arms around her middle. She held her dagger in her right hand, the blade flat against her arm and out of sight. "Go," she whispered, and Abby began to half-drag her "drunken shipmate" across the deck.

"'Ere, wot's this row?" the guard enquired, holding his lantern aloft to make out the two people coming toward him.

"Too much ale," Colleen mumbled. "Gotta relieve me bladder, and 'e's 'elpin' me."

"I'll bet 'e's 'elpin'," the old sailor said with a snicker. He was one of the crew who frequently made use of the little cabin boy to vent some of his frustrations during long nights at sea and knew how "helpful" the boy was. He turned back to the railing and once again sought the sailor on the pier, when it came to him that the clothing the cabin boy wore was not what it should have been. He turned back toward the duo, saying, "'Ey, wot's—"

Colleen clamped a hand over his mouth and pushed her dagger up under his ribs. He grunted once and collapsed. Colleen supported his body so it didn't make a sound hitting the deck, and the two women dragged him to the side of the ship and covered him with a canvas sail.

"Help me get the gangplank in place," Colleen whispered, leading Abby to where it lay on the deck. Colleen picked up the guard's lantern and waved it to indicate to James that all was under control on the ship, then the two women lifted the plank out and dropped it in place. James made sure it was secure on the pier and waved to indicate they could come over. "That's Mr. Henry down there," she said softly. "Get off the ship now. I'll come and join you as soon as I have taken care of things here."

"What is it you plan to do?" Abby said in a whisper as Colleen ushered her toward the wooden walkway.

"I plan to blow this loathesome vessel into pieces and send her and her thieving crew to the bottom of the sea."

"Oh, please, don't do that. I beg you. I've come to know some of the crew in these past days, and there are those on board who were pressed into the service against their will. They should not pay the price with the pirates. And there is at least one woman who is … like us. I would hate to see her killed. Would it be possible to capture the pirates instead and perhaps free those who are also here against their will?"

"Abby, it would be impossible to separate the evil from the good and—"

"Please, Col. Cripple the ship and have the authorities arrest the pirates, can't you? Let a judge determine who should be punished and to what extent."

"That would be hard. I can't be sure she won't go down to the bottom like a rock with all hands on board."

"Please. Just try to prevent her sinking. Or perhaps I could find Mary—the one who goes by the name of Mark on the ship—and tell her she needs to get off the ship before you set off the charges."

"Oh, no. You have to get off the ship well before I light the powder. If you can tell me where I can find this Mary I'll see what I can do."

Abby threw her arms around Colleen's shoulders and kissed her firmly on the mouth.

Colleen was so surprised, she simply stood there blinking for a moment before she could move.

"Mary sleeps in an alcove near the entrance to the hold. I thought it was so she could keep an eye on me, but I suspect it was more for privacy from the men on board. I'm fairly certain you'll find her there, and if you tell her who you are, she'll know you've come to rescue me."

"What's to prevent her from rousing the entire ship?"

"She wants to be free of this life, to have a chance for happiness with a woman like us. I'm sure she'll be grateful for the opportunity to escape. She's not a bad person, really. Anne is another sort, but Mary cares for her, so if she can be spared also, it would be wonderful."

Colleen sighed, but she knew she would do what she could to ease Abby's mind about the two women. "I'll talk to Mary. If I get the feeling she's going to try to prevent me from blowing up the ship, I'll have no choice but to silence her. I'll try, that's all I can promise."

"Thank you." Abby kissed Colleen's lips softly, cupping her cheek in her hand. "I knew you would rescue me. And I know you will do what you can for Mary and Anne."

"Ah, don't count yourself rescued just yet. We still need to get you off this ship. And you must tell Mr. Henry to bring the navy and any other authorities he can round up to be here when the ship blows. Will you do that?"

"Yes, but ... I don't want to leave you," Abby said, her voice frightened.

"Please ... I have to make sure they can't come after us, and I don't wish to be worried about you while I'm doing it. It'll only be a few minutes, I promise. Go—I shall be along soon." Colleen pressed her lips to Abby's and marveled at how right the world seemed just to be able to reconnect with the woman she loved. She broke off the kiss and gazed into Abby's eyes for just a moment before turning her and giving her a little push toward the gangplank. Abby had not taken more than a few steps before Colleen caught up with her and whispered, "Perhaps you should remove your shoes. You still clump about in those rather loudly."

Abby kicked the loose-fitting shoes off, glad to be rid of them.

"Now off with you. Don't forget the shoes! Young Gordon would be quite upset if I lost his extra pair." Abby clutched the shoes against her chest and reluctantly made her way down the plank. James met her and ushered her to a spot behind a pole from which she could see what was happening on deck but be fairly invisible from the ship.

Colleen recovered her box and withdrew from it the cloth bundles she had sewn together. Her preparations also included separating strands of hemp rope and soaking them thoroughly with whale oil. One end of each strand of rope was sewn into one of the cloth sacks, leaving a few yards of rope hanging out to be used as a wick.

She threw a rope ladder over the side of the ship beside the nearest cannon and lowered herself to within a foot of the water. One of the bundles was clutched between her teeth, and in her hand, she held a canvas wrap that contained several large pieces of tar she'd picked up on the beach. Being careful to avoid getting the sticky tar on her hands, she pressed several chunks on the side of the ship, and to the lowest one, she stuck two of the sacks. She climbed back up the ladder and as she rose, she stuck the rope into the tar to keep it in place. When she reached the deck again, she moved farther forward and performed the same exercise two more times. After affixing the last bundles, she walked toward the front of the ship as far as the wick would allow, and there she stuck a final piece of tar with the rope imbedded in it.

Once everything was in place, Colleen crept to the nook on deck where Abby said she might find Mary. As she got close, she could hear soft snores, which she hoped belonged to Abby's friend. If not, she had another problem on her hands. Since she could not be sure what reception she would receive in any case, she drew her knife and held it near the sleeping woman's throat. She whispered, "Mary, wake up."

"Wha? Huh?" Mary sat up and felt the pinch of a knife against her neck, and before she could make another sound, a hand was placed firmly over her mouth.

"Quiet. If you try to rouse the ship I'll cut your throat. I'm Colleen Edwards. Abby asked me if I would spare you and your friend when I send this tub to the bottom. If you want to live, I suggest you do as I say. I'm going to pull the knife away from your throat, but it will not be so far away that I can't take you down in an instant. Will you be quiet?" Mary nodded, and Colleen removed her hand slowly from Mary's mouth.

Mary flexed her jaw and put her hand up to her neck to find a tiny trickle of blood. She looked into Colleen's face and knew the woman was dead serious about killing her, and she had no doubt she was also capable of sinking the ship with all hands on board.

"So you're lucky Colleen. I've no wish to meet Davy Jones, so please thank Abby for me."

Colleen nodded. "Done. Now if you can tell me where I might find your lady friend, I'll see about getting her to safety, as well."

Mary shook her head and frowned. "I'm afraid that won't be so easy. She sleeps in Calico Jack's cabin, and he's a restless sleeper. Vicious as well."

Colleen slid down the wall to sit beside Mary while she thought about what to do. At last she asked, "Can she swim, do you know?"

"Aye, she's more than a fair swimmer. Can't say the same for meself."

"Right then, we'll have to lower the jolly boat for you. If she's lucky, she'll survive the explosion and you can fish her out of the water. It's the best I can do, Mary."

Mary's eyes widened with alarm. "I know you have no reason to trust me, Colleen, but I can't get off this ship without at least trying to rouse her, as well. She's—well, pregnant. I would hate to think of her having to try to swim, especially if she's hurt when you scuttle this blasted vessel. Please—give me a few minutes to fetch her, and we will be off."

"By yourself? Not likely. We'll go together. You wake your friend and I'll deal with Calico Jack. Lead the way to his cabin, and remember, I'm only a breath behind you with a very sharp knife." Mary nodded and rose with Colleen following.

Colleen pulled a marlinspike from a coil of rope as the two women crept silently toward the pirate captain's cabin. When Mary nodded toward his door, Colleen took a firm grip on the marlinspike and indicated with a nod that Mary should open the door. Mary stepped inside and waited silently by the door as Colleen followed. An oil lamp guttered on Jack's desk so the room was not in total darkness. Colleen could easily make out the two forms on the bed in the corner, and the distinct sounds of snoring indicated neither had been disturbed by their entrance.

Mary knew Anne slept on the edge of the bed closest to the

door since Jack superstitiously refused to sleep without a solid wall at his back. Motioning for Colleen to go toward the far corner of the bed, Mary made her way to the near edge and knelt down. She was just about to touch Anne to wake her up when she realized there was only one person snoring now.

Jack sat up in bed, uncertain what had roused him, but knowing something was amiss. He turned toward the door and could not fail to see Mary where she crouched by the bed. A scowl crossed his features as the thought entered his mind that perhaps his suspicions that Read and Anne were having an affair behind his back were true, but before a word could form on his lips, Colleen brought the marlinspike down on his head. With a groan, he fell back onto the bed, unconscious.

"That's for my father," Colleen said. "Be grateful Abby was still alive or you'd be dead now." Colleen tucked the marlinspike into her waistband and knelt down to where Mary was still trying to wake Anne.

Anne was just coming around, and when she saw Colleen's face looking down at her, she yelped. A second later, Mary's hand covered her mouth.

"Shh, Anne, we have to get off the ship," Mary whispered. "This is Abby's Colleen, and she's got this tub rigged to blow."

"The hell you say," Anne said when Mary removed her hand from Anne's mouth. Anne jutted out her chin stubbornly and hunkered down in bed. "And what have you done to Jack? He'll kill you when he—"

"It's me you need to worry about killing you if you don't get up and out of here. Mary wanted to save you, but I'll leave you for the fish to feed on if you don't get moving." The glint in Colleen's eyes showed she meant business, and reluctantly Anne climbed out of bed.

"Let me get dressed at least. "

"Grab what you can carry and come on," Colleen said with more than a little hint of irritation in her voice. Colleen hooked her arm through Anne's and pulled her forward, even as Anne was clutching at her small sea chest. Her share of the booty they had amassed was far more important than something to wear. Mary made a grab for the chest she knew Jack kept a stash of coins in, and the threesome made their way to the starboard side of the boat.

"The Royal Navy will be on their way here soon, so we need to get you two off this ship," Colleen said. Together they lowered the jolly boat, and first Anne, then Mary climbed over the side and slid down a rope, dropping soundlessly into the boat. Mary waved at Colleen when she was ready to grip the oars and row, and Colleen waved back, whispering, "Good luck," under her breath.

Colleen went to the leeward side of the ship where she left the watchman's lantern, still lit. She removed the chimney from the lantern and set the rope alight.

Carrying the lantern, Colleen ran down the gangplank, waving for James to come and help her remove the plank. They pulled the heavy board onto the pier and cut the ropes tethering the ship. Using long poles, they pushed the ship until she began to drift away from shore. Colleen knew from the many times they'd called at this port that there was an underwater canyon not far out from shore. If the ship drifted long enough to reach deep water before the powder blew, it would be unlikely any man aboard would live to plunder another ship. She cocked her arm back and threw the lantern onto the deck of the ship, and the flames began to spread like lava. The noise might rouse some of the men perhaps, but they'd been drinking fairly heavily that day, so she took a chance that none of them would know what happened until it was too late to do anything but swim for safety. She did not dwell on what might happen to those who could not swim.

At the sound of footsteps clattering over the wooden planks of the pier, Colleen turned to see a dozen or more of the Royal Navy approaching. Thinking she'd only given James a short time to arrange for reinforcements to arrive, she turned to her father's next in command and clapped him on the shoulder. "Remind me to have my father give you a raise in pay, Mr. Henry."

"Aye, Cap'n, I'll do that," he said with a grin. He beamed at her as if she were the cleverest woman in the world. And in truth, in the man's experience, she probably was. Colleen beckoned for Abby to come out from hiding, and all three of them turned toward the blazing vessel, where forms could now be seen—many of them in flames—leaping over the side. That sight galvanized Colleen into action.

"Come. We need to get away from the pier before the powder explodes." Colleen took Abby's hand and began to run. They'd almost reached the warehouse where the young sailor was tied up when the first explosion shattered the night. "Yes," Colleen said with a satisfied grin on her face. She turned back to where the ship was now almost engulfed in flames, and the second explosion occurred. The vessel was beginning to list to the side, taking on water, as she'd hoped. "Mr. Henry, I'm going to take Lord Hume's daughter back to the *Betsy Ann* so she can get some rest without constant fear for her life. She will be in the captain's quarters and should not be disturbed for any reason. Oh, and I would be grateful if you would untie that young lad over yonder. Make sure to tell him that his kindness to a stranger is what gave him the gift of his life this night. And if he's smart, he'll use his gift wisely and stay as far away as he can from the likes of Calico Jack. If he wishes to earn an honest wage, we can take him on for the return journey."

"Aye, Cap'n. She'll not be disturbed, nor will yerself. Ye've barely slept the last days and nights and must be wicked tired. I'll take care of yon lad and stay here about, just to make sure them pirates who manage to come ashore are locked up good and proper."

"God bless you, Mr. Henry. I could not have done this without you." She grasped his hand to shake it, then thought better of it, and pulled him in for a hug instead. "The smartest thing my father ever did was hire you," she said with a smile as they pulled apart. Embarrassed, he shuffled off in the direction of the captive sailor, and Colleen grasped Abby's hand again. "Come with me, love. Mr. Henry is right. I'm falling down weary, and you must be, as well, after your ordeal. We'll rest tonight and in the morning decide what our next steps should be." Hand in hand, they walked toward the *Betsy Ann*.

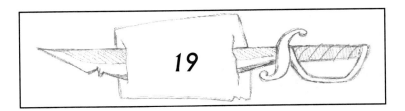

19

Colleen used a faggot to light the lamp in her father's quarters. As it flared, the neat space came into view, and Colleen stepped aside to allow Abby to enter. "Welcome to the *Betsy Ann*. I hope you don't find it too cramped."

"Colleen, I've spent the better part of a week in a hold with who knows what sort of vermin and filth. This is beautiful. More so because you're here." She turned toward Colleen and smiled, but the smile faded when she saw the shocked expression on Colleen's face. "What is it, love? You look as if you've seen a ghost."

Colleen gently took Abby's chin in her hand and turned her face toward the light. A fading purple bruise marred her cheek, and smudges of dirt streaked her lovely skin. Colleen lightly kissed the bruise before pulling away and looking into Abby's eyes. "Who gave you this bruise?"

Abby's fingers flew to her cheek, and she touched the spot where moments before Colleen's lips had been. "Oh, I'd forgotten about that. One of Jack Rackham's thugs thought I should be still, and I was of another opinion. I'm afraid he won the argument." She hastened to add, "But no other harm came to me. Mary saw to that. She truly did look after me."

"Then I'm grateful you persuaded me to spare her life. I hope she fares well. And I hope you'll not take this the wrong way, but I believe you are in need of a bit of cleaning up. Will you be able to manage a sponge bath by yourself? I know you're used to having your maid help you. "

Abby playfully slapped Colleen on the arm. "Do you think I'm a helpless babe, Col? I'm perfectly capable of bathing myself. Now if you'll just fill up a tub with some perfumed hot water and help me undo the strange nautical fastenings on these clothes—"

"Oh, sorry, we have no cook on board, thus the stove is not heated. I'm afraid the water will have to be cold. But I'll gladly assist you with removing your clothes, then take myself to the other side of the cabin to allow you some privacy." At Abby's nod, Colleen reached to the snaps that held the trousers up and loosened them.

Abby grasped the top of the garment to prevent it from sliding to the floor. A part of her was eager to be naked in Colleen's presence, but she didn't want it to be when she was caked in filth.

Colleen removed a small flannel sheet from a cupboard and handed it to Abby. "I'll fetch some water. This sheet will cover you while you bathe." Colleen took her own nightshirt from beneath her father's pillow and handed that to Abby, as well. "This will be much too long for you, but it is all I have."

Abby clutched the garment to her breast, noting the unmistakable scent of Colleen that clung to it. She could not suppress a smile as she thought about the skin this shirt had caressed. "This will be perfect, thank you."

"Good. Well, let me get that water then. I'll be back in a trice." Colleen stepped out the door and closed it softly behind her.

Abby slid her feet out of the clunky shoes before allowing the trousers to slip to the floor. The rest of the clothes followed in short order, and she sat at the chair in front of Colleen's father's desk with the sheet firmly wrapped around her. A short time later, Colleen returned with two nearly full buckets of water, which she placed on the floor near Abby's feet.

Colleen withdrew a cake of soap from a pouch about her waist and handed it to Abby. "It's French milled soap." Abby sniffed it and smiled. "Glad it meets with your approval. Now if you need anything else, I'll be on my father's bunk. I'll face the wall so please feel free to—well, just feel free." Colleen sat on the edge of the bunk and pulled off her boots, which she tossed under the desk. She lay down and rolled onto her side, her mind full of thoughts about what Abby was doing only a few feet away.

Abby squealed when the cold water touched her skin. Even though she assured Colleen she was able to bathe herself, she could not remember a time when she had done so. And she knew she was making a mess with the water but was not sure what to do to prevent it. At last, she simply let the water pool at her feet, determined that she would mop it up when she was finished.

When Abby was satisfied she had removed the grime from her body, she dried off with the sheet, then, after donning the nightshirt, she used the sheet to sop up the puddles on the floor. Not sure what to do with it after that, she draped it over the back of the chair, then made her way to the side of the bunk. True to her word, Colleen was facing the wall. As Abby got closer, she could hear the even sounds of her breathing and knew Colleen was asleep. Knowing the way she pushed herself to reach Port Royal in the length of time she had, Abby was loath to disturb Colleen's slumber. Instead, she extinguished the lamp and gently crawled up from the foot of the bunk to lie with her back against the wall. With a sigh, she curled up against Colleen, feeling safe and secure for the first time in a long time, and in a few moments, she joined her lover in sleep.

Colleen awoke the following morning just as the sun was painting the sky with bright crimson and orange. She was fully dressed but for her boots and lying in the captain's bunk. Abby's head was tucked under her chin, her arm wrapped firmly around Colleen's middle and her leg on top of Colleen's thigh. Colleen began to stroke the soft blond hair that spilled over her chest. With a little moan, Abby snuggled closer. Emboldened, Colleen traced her finger around Abby's very kissable mouth, and Abby sighed as she parted her lips. Colleen put her fingers under Abby's chin and tilted her head up to look into her precious face. Abby's eyelids fluttered and opened, and her face brightened at the sight that greeted her.

"Good morning, my captain," she said, laughing.

"Good morning, my lady," Colleen returned, and she lowered her head to brush her lips softly over Abby's mouth. "I have so longed to wake to your presence in my bed that I fear this is all a dream."

"Is it possible for two people to share the exact same dream? Because that's been my wish, as well, and now here we are. I shall pinch you, and you can pinch me to see if we're truly awake." And she reached out and pinched the skin under Colleen's rib. Colleen squirmed; Abby had found her ticklish spot. She grasped Abby's hand to stop the tickling and brought it to her mouth to kiss the palm.

"I would rather kiss than pinch to see if you're dreaming. Would that meet with your approval?" She kissed Abby's wrist, then the bend in her elbow. At last, she turned to her face and began to rain kisses upon her cheeks, her nose, and finally her lips.

"Yes. Oh, yes," Abby said when Colleen pulled away again. "Your kiss is like nothing I ever hoped to experience ... soft, yet firm, giving ... and taking. I could kiss you forever."

"And would you also let me touch your body ... kiss you all over and, I hope, please you in ways you have not imagined?"

"Forever," she replied unhesitatingly. "Provided I am allowed the same liberties with you."

"I could not refuse you anything, my love."

Abby's face lit up with a wicked grin. "Good. Then remove that shirt, as well as the bindings from your breasts, so I might feel the fullness of them against me." Obediently, Colleen untangled herself from Abby's body and stood beside the bed. She unfastened the buttons of the shirt and drew it down her arms, tossing the garment onto the chair by the small desk. She took up her knife and cut the threads that held the bandage, then slowly unwrapped the cloth. Abby could not take her eyes off Colleen as more of her skin was revealed. She licked her lips unconsciously, and Colleen smiled down at her. Finally, Colleen dropped the cloth to the floor and stood in nothing but her trousers.

"Will that be all, my lady?" she said seductively. She was surprised at the sound of her own voice; never in her life had she sounded like that. But then, never before did she have reason to.

"The ... trousers, too, Colleen. I wish to see all of you." Abby's voice was deeper than normal and heavy with desire. Colleen untied the cord that secured the trousers about her waist and allowed her pants to drop to the floor. She stepped out and stood naked for the first time in front of anyone since her mother bathed her as a child.

"My lady, I would like to gaze upon you, as well. May I help you remove your nightshirt?"

"Yes, please." Colleen held out her hand to help Abby sit up on the bed. When she did so, she felt Abby trembling.

"Are you cold?" Colleen asked softly, concern in her voice. Abby shook her head no. Colleen slowly drew the shirt up Abby's body and over her head. "Oh" was all she could say when she saw Abby's breasts, and a few moments later, when speech returned, she added, "Beautiful ... you're breathtaking, my lady." Now it was Colleen whose face shone with desire as she viewed the curves and valleys before her.

Colleen closed the scant distance between them; her eyes shut and a moan escaped her lips at the first touch of Abby's breasts against her ribcage. She dipped her head and met Abby's lips, at the same time wrapping her arms around her small frame and pulling her fully against her body.

"Oh, God..." Abby groaned when they broke apart to gasp in some much needed air. "I want ... oh, I want to feel you against me, inside me ... everywhere. I don't have the words to say what I feel, but my body is responding to your touch like the strings of a violin in the hands of a master."

"I want to please you, my lady. Do you trust me? I have an idea that I may hurt you a bit, but I hope the small pain will be worth it." Living aboard ship a good deal of her life, Colleen had heard sailors speak of their encounters with women. She liked to lie in the jolly boat at night and watch the stars, and she could hear her shipmates talk. Their words were crude; they did not realize the captain's daughter could hear. For the most part, it was clear they did not give a fig about pleasuring the women they bedded. It was all about what the women could do for them. And she knew there was pain for a woman when she was deflowered, but all the men made it seem as if the women were well pleased when the flower was plucked. One or two of the more considerate men spoke of ways to arouse and please women, with their hands and mouths, and Colleen listened. She even tried some of the things on herself and was surprised to feel a pleasant explosion beyond anything she'd felt before. She hoped to employ the techniques her shipmates had described to give the same pleasant feeling to Abby.

"I trust you with my life, my body ... everything I am or ever hope to be."

Colleen picked Abby up and cradled her in her arms for a moment before gently laying her on the bed. She then crawled onto the bed and slowly moved up Abby's body, allowing her breasts to brush against the soft flesh of Abby's torso until they were touching those of the woman beneath her. Both women's nipples were immediately hard as pebbles. Colleen used her knee to part Abby's legs and settled her thigh between them, feeling the heat and wetness that emanated from her center.

Abby gasped when she felt Colleen's leg against her mound. She lightly trailed her fingers down Colleen's sides, marveling at the contrast between soft skin and taut muscles. Her hands stopped at Colleen's thighs, and without even realizing she was doing it, she pulled her even closer to her body. Colleen kissed her mouth, her tongue gently begging entrance, and Abby complied. She traced the contours of Abby's lips with her tongue before beginning to explore her mouth. Tentatively, Abby touched her tongue to Colleen's, growing bolder as Colleen responded with a moan deep in her throat. When Abby sucked the tip of Colleen's tongue, Colleen thought she would die from the sheer joy of the feeling.

"Oh, Abby," she gasped. "I want ... God, I don't have words for this, either. I feel that my heart will burst out of my chest from pure happiness." She took Abby's hand and placed it on her breast. "Feel how my heart hammers."

Abby smiled; she could indeed feel the steady beat of Colleen's heart. She also felt the lushness of her breast, and her fingers began to knead the soft flesh.

She pinched the nipple between her fingers until Colleen could take no more of the tender assault and grasped her hand. "You make me insane with wanting you, Abby. But please, let me love you first. I want to fill you, taste you. Then you can do as you like with me. My body screams with the desire to make love to you."

"Yes ... make love to me. But know that I suffer the same agonies as you, and bear with me if I give in to temptation. You are a powerful and beautiful woman, my captain. I can't resist you."

Colleen smiled as she put Abby's hands together and grasped them in one of her own. "Perhaps this will keep your hands from mischief..." But she failed to realize that as she rose up to take hold of Abby's hands, her breasts were brought within reach of Abby's mouth, and Abby was quick to take advantage of the situation. Her tongue made a circle around Colleen's nipple, then she drew it into her mouth. "Oh, dear God," Colleen rasped. She shuddered and pressed her breast into Abby's mouth, and her lover took it hungrily. With great restraint, Colleen pulled away, sliding down so her breasts were no longer a temptation. Colleen placed a trail of kisses down Abby's neck and shoulders, and when she reached her breasts, she snaked out her tongue and licked between them. She cupped both breasts in her hands, licking each one in turn until the skin around the nipple was drawn up into a tiny mass of bumps. Then she pulled first one nipple, then the other into her mouth, sucking and taking tiny nips with her teeth. Abby bucked underneath her, grinding her mound against Colleen, striving for contact. Colleen reluctantly let go of the succulent nipples and continued to move down the exquisite body. She could smell Abby's arousal, and it made her insane to touch her there. But she knew she had to be gentle to avoid causing injury to her inexperienced lover.

Colleen moved lower still, her tongue tracing the line that joined Abby's thigh with her body. She licked down the inside of her thigh, pushing her legs farther apart to give her full access to her lush body. She could see the pearls of moisture clinging to Abby's coral-colored lips, and after licking her way back up Abby's other thigh, she paused at last before her center. "May I kiss you here?" she said softly.

Abby sighed. "I think I shall die if you don't."

That was all Colleen needed to know. With a sigh, she reached out her tongue to part the folds and was rewarded with a shuddering moan as Abby ground herself into her. Colleen had no idea exactly what it was she was supposed to do once she got here ... her shipmates had not shared that much detail for her to overhear. But it seemed she did not need to know; Abby was showing by her motions and little sighs what felt good to her.

The muscles of Colleen's stomach clenched, and her own womanhood throbbed as her tongue explored the glorious treasure offered her. She brought her finger to the moist folds and teased it toward Abby's opening. She inserted it inside the depths that beckoned her, only to the middle of her finger, then made as if to withdraw it. Abby's hand found her own and held it in place. "Please, I want to have you inside me.... You'll not hurt me. I need ... Ohh." At her urging, Colleen once again inserted the finger until it met some resistance, whereupon she pushed as gently as she could until she felt the resistance tear. At that same moment, she renewed her licking of the taut bundle of nerves that peeked out of the folds of skin, and as she hoped, Abby seemed to feel the pleasure of that and not the pain of the rupturing of her maidenhead.

Colleen dropped off the narrow bed onto her knees and drew Abby to the edge of the bed, draping her legs over her shoulders. She put her arms underneath Abby's thighs and pulled her even closer. She filled her with a second finger and heard the moan that signaled it was a welcome feeling. Her tongue continued to worship the nub, which fairly quivered at the attention.

Suddenly, Abby's head began to thrash from side to side, her fingers spasmodically clenching at the blankets. She thrust herself into Colleen as if her very life depended on the contact, and with her heels planted on Colleen's back, she pushed herself up until Colleen had to stretch to maintain the connection.

From her own experiments on herself, Colleen knew that what was needed now was speed, and she redoubled her efforts with her fingers and her mouth. Abby moaned, saying, "oh, oh, oh, oh," as if it were a mantra, the last "oh" very nearly a scream as she toppled over the edge into an ecstasy she never thought she would know. When she could take no more, she collapsed back onto the bed, tears leaking unknown and unbidden from her eyes.

Colleen crawled up on the bed, kissing the tears from her cheeks as she softly asked, "Are you well, my lady? Have I hurt you after all?"

"No, not a bit.... Please, believe me. I've never in my life felt anything so wonderful as what you just did. I have no idea why I'm crying, but it's not from pain." Abby pulled Colleen against her body, craving the contact, and a shudder rippled through her as she seemed to feel once again the explosion that had rocked her moments before. "I want to give you those feelings, as well, my captain. Truly, it must be one of the greatest gifts one can give to someone they love."

"I am yours to do with as you will, but you need not do anything to please me. Loving you has been the greatest pleasure I could imagine."

"And I want to feel that pleasure, as well." Abby grasped Colleen's shoulders and gently pushed her off her body and onto her back. She rolled on top of her until she felt the length of their bodies touching. As Colleen had done, she used her leg to part her lover's legs and settled her body into the welcoming V. Their damp mounds touched, and Colleen groaned. Abby kissed her, tasting her own musky wetness on Colleen's lips. Colleen's mouth opened in welcome and Abby deepened the kiss, hearing the growls of pleasure coming from her. Instinct guided her hands and mouth as she moved down Colleen's body, kissing her shoulders, her neck, and the soft swells of her breasts. Her tongue painted a trail of goose flesh over the quivering skin of Colleen's belly. Her hands were busy kneading the mounds of her breasts and pinching the nipples until Colleen once again thought she could not take another moment. She groaned and thrust against Abby, silently begging for her to take the next step. Abby responded by moving up the muscular body and taking her nipple into her mouth. Her tongue teased the tip until it was a pebble in her mouth, then she moved to the other breast, achieving the same result.

"Please..." Colleen begged at last. Her body was quivering as if she were freezing cold, and she knew if she didn't soon feel Abby's hands and mouth on her sex, she would go mad. "I need you ... touch me ... or I shall scream and wake the whole town."

Abby chuckled and rose up to look into Colleen's face. Her hand trailed down the long body underneath her until it reached the damp mound. She parted the lips with her finger and insinuated the digit inside. Immediately, the walls of Colleen's center closed about the finger, holding it inside, grasping as if it would never release its prisoner. "Is this what you wanted to feel?" Colleen nodded. "And this?" Abby asked, inserting yet another finger.

"God, yes! How you excite me, Abby...."

"I've barely begun. I intend to drive you mad with desire before I allow you to experience the wonder you visited upon me." Abby once again slid down Colleen's body, never stopping the motion of her fingers within the damp cave that held them. She stopped with her mouth just above the thatch of dark hair and inhaled the musky scent. Her mouth watered at the thought of tasting what waited for her just a few inches away. Without warning, she withdrew her fingers and used both hands to gently pry open the lips she longed to kiss. She lowered her head and licked from the bottom of the opening to the top, then back down again. Her fingers held the lips open as far, and she thrust her tongue into the opening and licked the inside of the walls. She pushed as much of her tongue inside as she could possibly manage, then withdrew all but the tip before pushing it in yet again.

Colleen's body bucked underneath her, and a sound almost inhuman began to build in her chest. "Please ... please ... please."

Without losing the rhythm she had established with her tongue, Abby withdrew it and quickly inserted two fingers again.

She sucked the swollen nub that had enlarged to twice its size into her mouth and flicked it with her tongue. It seemed only a moment had passed before Colleen thrust hard against her mouth and called out her name. But Abby didn't stop until Colleen put her hands under her arms and pulled her up her body to rest on her chest. She could feel the hammering of Colleen's heart against her cheek and wrapped her arms around Colleen's neck until her heartbeat and breathing slowed to a normal pace.

"Were you pleased, my captain?" she inquired. Colleen could only sigh and crush her tightly against her chest.

"Could you not tell? It was the most glorious thing I ever felt."

"I felt no resistance when my fingers entered you," Abby said. "Has someone before me shared a bed with you?" She realized she was jealous of whoever it might have been who had knowledge of Colleen's body.

Colleen laughed. "No, 'twas naught but my own hand that did the deed. It is not in my nature to love a man. But I yearned to feel what my shipmates told me they had seen in the faces of the women they had loved when the little death was upon them."

"And were you able to bring yourself to that place? Was it more pleasurable than what I have done?" Abby's tone was light, but the expression on her face betrayed her uncertainty as to the true depths of Colleen's satisfaction with her efforts.

Noting the flicker of uncertainty as it swept across Abby's face, Colleen smiled and took hold of her hand, kissing the palm, then placing the hand upon her still racing heart. "It's like saying if one has been caught in a summer shower, one knows what it feels like to be in the heart of a hurricane. I have experienced the awesome power of a tropical storm. Believe me, the small pleasures I have given myself in the past are but a mist ... you have given me the hurricane."

"Oh, my bonny lass, it delights me to know I have pleased you well. I knew from almost the first moment I clapped eyes on you that you were the one I could give my heart to. But I had no idea two women could find ways to...." She shrugged, unable to find words to adequately describe what she had just experienced.

"Nor did I, but I was damned well going to keep trying until I figured it out. But only with you, my love. No woman I met before you inspired such feelings in me."

"Then we are a pair, indeed. I can't imagine feeling such closeness with another, be it man or woman. You are the one who completes me, Colleen."

Abby snuggled into Colleen's shoulder, their arms and legs entwined. Soon both women were once again asleep, their faces still bearing the smiles they could not seem to wipe off.

When Colleen awoke again it was mid-afternoon, and she tried to identify the sound that had roused her. Just then, Abby's stomach growled, and Colleen knew it was the soft rumbling that pulled her from slumber. It occurred to her to wonder when Abby took her last meal. She didn't think to ask in the midst of rescuing her, nor later in the heat of passion. She tightened her arm around Abby's shoulders and leaned down to kiss her cheek. "Abby, wake up, love. We need to get you something to eat before your grumbling stomach scares all the fish away."

"Bloody ha-ha," Abby muttered, snuggling more deeply into Colleen's shoulder.

Colleen laughed. "You talk like a sailor, Abby. What would your father think if he heard you talking like that?"

"I'm sure I don't care. He can think what he likes. I want to stay here with you—just like this." She lowered her head to Colleen's soft breast and drew the nipple into her mouth. As it hardened, she felt a flood of wetness coat her own thighs and marveled at the power this woman had to turn her into a quivering mass of jelly merely by her proximity.

Colleen groaned at the delicious feel of the talented mouth on her breast, and through clenched teeth, she said, "Are you sure you wouldn't like to get something to eat?"

"Yes, I would." Abby rose up on her knees, then threw her leg over Colleen's middle. When her liberally coated sex came into contact with Colleen's abdomen, she squirmed underneath her. "Feel what you do to me, Col, without even touching me. Imagine how wet I'm going to be when I taste you."

"Oh, Abby. You are so wet. I want to taste you as well. Please, shift around so that you are within reach of my mouth and your head is between my—oh!" Abby quickly turned around and scooted up until her knees were just above Colleen's shoulders. Colleen wrapped her arms around the lovely derrière and pulled down until Abby's sex was within reach of her tongue. The scent alone was enough to drive her nearly mad with wanting. She parted the folds and eagerly lapped up the musky wetness.

Abby plunged her face between Colleen's thighs but found her goal was just out of reach. Undaunted, she grabbed a pillow and said, "Raise up your bum so I can put this under you." When Colleen did as requested, her swollen lips were just where Abby wanted them. "Oh, yes," she whispered as she reached her tongue out to the tantalizing flesh.

If asked, they could not have told you where one of them began and the other started; they were as one. When one needed a bit more pressure, the other seemed to know instinctively and provide what was needed. If one was too fast or too slow or too hard or too soft, she would adjust until they both began to climb together toward an orgasm that struck both simultaneously and left them breathless, unable to move.

After what felt like an eternity, Abby was able to collect enough strength to turn herself upright and lay her head once again on Colleen's breast. "How on earth could you know to do that?" she asked, unable to fathom the depths of her lover's skills.

"I ... well, I heard some of the lads talking about doing something similar with their ladies. I reckoned if they could manage it, so could we." It occurred to her to wonder if Abby were able to achieve an orgasm, and she asked softly, "Were you not pleased? I could certainly…"

Abby chuckled. "Rest easy, my captain. I was more than pleased. I just have to express my amazement at how skilled you have become in such a short span of time. If it were up to me, we would still be holding hands and sharing stolen glances."

Colleen tipped Abby's chin up and placed a kiss on lips that were slightly bruised and swollen. "I think you would have reached the same place in no time, love. I simply had the small advantage of overhearing my shipmates talking about the mechanics of it.

But I have no doubt that our combined excitement would have driven us to this point without any tutoring whatever. And now, what do you say to a bit of breakfast? I've worked up quite an appetite myself, and I know you have, as well."

"All right, but I think it's supper time by now."

At the mention of the word supper, Abby's stomach made a noise unlike anything Colleen had heard before. "Good God, I think we'd better appease this beast before it consumes us both." She rolled out of bed and held out her hand to draw Abby to her feet. "Let me dress quickly, and I will see if I can find something more appropriate for you to wear than trousers." Without bothering to bind her breasts, she pulled her trousers and shirt on and left the cabin in her bare feet.

Without Colleen's solid body to warm her, Abby felt a bit of a chill, and she pulled the blanket off the bed and wrapped it around herself. She walked to the desk where Colleen's father must have spent many hours and wondered what the man would be like. The man who raised such a gorgeous creature as Colleen was someone she wanted to meet. Abby looked up at the sound of the door opening to find Colleen standing there with a beautiful blue gown draped over one arm and petticoats and a corset in the other.

"I'm afraid it will be awfully long for you, but perhaps while I'm gathering something for us to eat, you can take up the hem a bit. Or simply hold it up so you don't trip, whichever suits you."

Abby took the garment from her arms and held it up to admire it. It was silk with lace around the sleeves and bodice, the stitches neater and more even than any dress she'd ever seen. "Oh, Colleen, what a gorgeous gown! Wherever did you get it so quickly?"

"It was—is mine. It was the last dress my mother made for me. I could not bear to part with it as I did the rest of my gowns. It was to be my coming-out dress. Seems a lifetime ago now." Tears brimmed in her eyes as she looked at the dress held in front of Abby's body. Finally, she pulled in a deep breath and brushed the tears out of her eyes. "Well, I suspect it will look much better on you than it ever would have on me. And I don't plan to ever wear a frock again in my life, if I can help it. So it's yours now. Think of it as a gift from my mother."

Abby clutched the dress to her chest, but when she felt her own tears begin to fall, she set it aside to avoid staining it with tears. She threw herself into Colleen's arms and hugged her with all her might. "Thank you so much for this gift. I will treasure it always. And when I wear it, I will think of your mother and imagine her working on it. Perhaps I will paint her portrait one day with this dress upon her lap."

"I look forward to seeing her again through your eyes. I have no doubt you can capture her essence as well as you catch the hues and life of the sea on canvas."

"I must hem the dress. I don't want to soil it by dragging the bottom in the dirt. Do you have a needle and some thread?"

Colleen withdrew a spool of thread and needle from her pocket. "I thought you might want to. If you'd like, I can pin it for you." At Abby's nod, Colleen pulled the chair away from her father's desk. She fitted the dress over Abby's head and settled it over her hips. If not for the length, it would have been a perfect fit. Colleen put her hands on Abby's waist and lifted her up on the chair. Pulling a pin cushion from another pocket, Colleen set to work pinning the hem. She was fast and efficient, and soon she was lifting Abby down from the chair. She carefully removed the dress to avoid pricking Abby and laid it out on her father's bed. "It seems you will need to wear Gordon's clothes for a while longer. I can't have you sitting around here with nothing on or you'll never get the dress hemmed or anything to eat." She waggled her eyebrows. Abby laughed; the sound was musical to Colleen's ears.

"If you say so, but you'll need to help me put it on. Honestly, I thought women had it hard with the clothes we wear, but this…" She picked up the clothes she had discarded the previous night and proceeded to pull on the trousers.

With only a few tickles and touches, Colleen helped Abby dress before withdrawing to see what she might pull together for them to eat. Her last sight as she walked out the door was of Abby seated in her father's chair, pulling needle and thread through the shimmering blue fabric, her eyes intent upon her task.

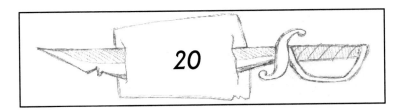

20

"Ship pullin' into the dock, Captain. She's flyin' a Bahamian flag," Gordon called as he came running up the gangplank. James gave the lad permission to go aboard only long enough to convey this important message. Nothing less than the approach of the governor could warrant disturbing Colleen. It was Saturday morning, the day the ransom was to be paid. Colleen was scraping the bits of food left on their breakfast dishes over the side when Gordon came on board. She was grateful he didn't arrive an hour or so earlier and come below decks to find her since she and Abby were once again engaged in their new favorite pastime. It mattered little to Colleen, but she feared it would have embarrassed Abby to be found in such a compromising position.

"Thank you, Gordon. Go tell the captain of yon vessel that Captain Charles Edwards the second will be calling within the hour to speak with his esteemed passenger."

"Aye, Captain." He turned and sped off again on his mission.

Abby was below deck putting the finishing touches on the hem while waiting for her father to arrive. In fact, she almost dreaded his coming. The time she and Colleen spent together alone aboard the *Betsy Ann* was the happiest of her life, and she was loath to see it end. When the door opened after a brief knock she looked up to see Colleen dressed in her father's uniform, her breasts bound for the first time in two days. Abby sighed. She knew this moment would arrive, but she didn't have to like it.

"Your father will be in port shortly," Colleen said softly. "If you're ready, I'll help you put on your dress." Wordlessly, Abby rose. She was already wearing the corset and petticoats, lacking only the dress to complete her wardrobe. Colleen had also found a pair of shoes that would do, but it was necessary to stuff quite a bit of cotton into the toes to keep them on her feet. Colleen settled the dress over Abby's head and fastened the buttons behind her. When she was finished, she turned Abby around and gasped at what a beautiful figure she made in that gown. Colleen could tell by the silence and the look on Abby's face that she was not looking forward to being restored to her family.

"So soon?" Abby sighed. "I suppose there's nothing for it but to return with him to Nassau, though God himself knows I would rather spend the rest of my days with you."

Colleen smiled and put her fingers under Abby's chin, raising her face so she could just see the tears gleaming in the corners of her eyes. She kissed her lightly on the lips and said, "I have a plan, my love. Perhaps you need not return with your father, if he agrees to my proposal. Follow my lead when we speak with him." Abby's face lit up at the prospect of remaining with Colleen.

"Anything ... just tell me what you want me to do."

Lord Hume paced nervously on the deck of the ship, awaiting the arrival of the captain of the *Betsy Ann*. He dared not hope the man had been successful in his quest, for if he allowed himself to believe only to find he'd failed, he was not certain his heart could survive it. He truly adored his only daughter and was nearly at his wit's end over this entire business. He vowed he would never allow her out of his sight again until she married, to prevent a recurrence. At the sound of footsteps on the wooden pier, he turned to see a tall man wearing the uniform of a captain, but certainly not the gentleman he'd met in Nassau. Beside him, her arm draped over his, walked his daughter, head high and a smile on her face. "Tell my wife to come up on deck," he asked a crewman, and with a bow, the man withdrew to do his bidding. Lord Hume almost ran down the gangplank to greet her, but such a display was not seemly to one of his station. Instead, he simply stood, his face wreathed in smiles, as Abby came aboard.

"Oh, Father!" she cried, launching herself into his arms. He pulled her close, and she smelled the faint tobacco scent that clung to his clothes. Much as she wanted to remain with Colleen, she was truly happy to see him.

"Thank God you're all right. Did they harm you, child?"

"No, Father. I have no doubt they would have, if Captain Edwards had not rescued me when ... he did." It was then that Lord Hume turned his attention to the man in the red coat and French cocked hat standing a discreet distance away.

"I met Captain Edwards in Nassau, and this most certainly is not him."

"You are correct, my lord. I am his son, Charles Edwards the second. I was attending to other business in Nassau when you met with my father."

"And where is your father then? I believe I owe him a reward for the safe return of my daughter." It was at that moment Lady Hume arrived on deck, and with a shriek, she clasped her daughter to her, sobbing, and the two women sat down, hugging and crying. Lord Hume glanced back at the handsome captain, awaiting an explanation.

"Alas, my father was wounded while attempting to remove your daughter from the ship. I had to put ashore and leave him in the care of a doctor. My sister is with him. I believe you met her in Nassau."

"That's it! I knew your face was familiar. You look just like her. I remember those piercing eyes."

"Our features are ... very similar, my lord. We take after our mother, God rest her soul."

"I am truly saddened to hear your father was hurt. Did they offer any hope for his survival?"

"Very little, I'm afraid, but while there is any hope at all, I shall cling to it. And I must return now that this unfortunate business is at an end and see how he fares."

"Then it is you who have saved my daughter from those cutthroats, and it is you who will be rewarded. The ransom I was prepared to pay will be yours." Colleen shook her head no, and the man looked at her in confusion. "I will gladly pay anything more you ask, only tell me what it is."

"I want no reward, unless you will call it a dowry. I ask for your daughter's hand in marriage, if you would agree, my lord. I love her with all my heart and would spend the rest of my days making her happy if you would grant me the honor of marrying her."

Abby heard the words, and separating herself from her mother's arms, she rushed to her father's side. "Oh, Father, please say yes. The captain has won my heart with his kind and gentle ways, and I know our lives would be filled with joy if we are married. Please, give us your blessing, Father."

Lord Hume was stunned. He had almost given up hope of his daughter marrying again. She had made it clear she would sooner die than marry again except for love. And she was twenty-three already, surely almost past the age when any man would have her. Lady Hume took her husband's arm and pulled him aside, whispering something in his ear. With a nod, he turned back to Colleen. "I agree, Captain. When we return to Nassau, we will begin to make the arrangements for the wedding."

"With all due respect, my lord, I would ask that we be wed here and now. The captain of this vessel can perform the ceremony provided we are on the high seas. I would have her with me as my bride when I return for my father. The uncertainty of the sea makes it difficult to know when I could come to Nassau for the wedding, and I'm impatient to enjoy the ... wonders of marriage that you and your wife share. I beg you, sir, please allow us to marry now." Abby stood next to Colleen and grasped her hand, twining their fingers together. She smiled brightly at Colleen, then to her father, pleading with her eyes for his agreement.

Lord and Lady Hume conversed quietly for several moments before His Lordship turned back to Colleen. "Sir, I have no idea how you have managed it, but you certainly seem to have captured her heart. I cannot refuse my daughter something she so obviously desires. We shall draw up the marriage contract today, and you may be wed tomorrow. Is that soon enough for you, young captain?"

"My lord, you have made me the happiest man alive. I promise you will not regret your decision."

"I am certain I will not, provided you and my daughter give me many grandsons." He clapped Colleen heartily on the back and fortunately did not appear to notice the blush that colored her cheeks.

"Er, yes, my lord. We will certainly try." And she winked at Abby, who blushed shyly.

Abby smiled at her father and said brightly, "Indeed, Father. If we do not have children, it will not be for lack of trying." She squeezed Colleen's fingers tightly.

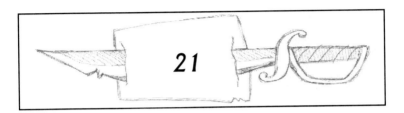

21

Emelia paced around the small room she and Abby were sharing near Port Royal. Abby would be married the next day, and the very thought of such short notice sent Emelia into fits, even though the news of the marriage itself—and to a captain at that—made her heart light. It was all she could do not to pick out names for the grandchildren on which she was already counting. "I simply cannot understand how your father could agree to let you get married so quickly. Why, I have no time at all to pick out a dress or to arrange for a celebration. Your aunts will be so disappointed not to have the opportunity to attend, not to mention—"

Abby cut off her mother before she could go through the entire argument again. "Mother, please, we've been through all this. I wish to be with Charles when he meets with the doctor who has been caring for his father. If the man is lost, Charles will need me for support. And if he lives, then I will get to meet my new father-in-law. Surely you can understand that. I'm sure my aunts will be happy enough to learn I've married, and their presence at the event would not do much to increase their happiness. As for a dress … I would be honored to marry in the dress Charles's mother made for his sister. It will seem as if she is there with us

Vada Foster

in spirit."

"Abigail, that dress is blue. Not at all appropriate for a wedding, beautiful though it may be. I spoke with a dressmaker, and he has a dress commissioned for another and never picked up, which might be altered to suit you. Without seeing you, of course, he cannot be certain. We need to go to his shop as soon as possible for a fitting." Arguing was pointless; Emelia was a force to be reckoned with when she had her mind set on something.

"Of course, Mother. Let's go now, and after we can meet Father and Charles in the dining room for dinner."

Pleased to at last be doing something positive toward making arrangements, Emelia smiled as she took Abby's elbow and propelled her out the door.

The dress was lovely and very nearly a perfect fit for Abby. The dressmaker, who was called Pierre the Pansy, fluttered around Abby gushing about what a beautiful bride she would be. The dress needed only a bit of alteration at the waist and shortening of the sleeves, and Pierre quickly pinned and marked the fabric where work was needed. When he was satisfied he had everything exactly right, he asked his assistant to take the dress off Abby and hang it upon a dressmaker's dummy. When Abby was once again dressed in her own clothes, Pierre approached her and whispered, "Cherie, you were the one being held by Calico Jack, no?"

"Yes. Yes, I was. How do you know this?"

He shrugged. "This is a small port. Everybody knows everything. But tell me, do you know if Anne Bonny and er Mark Read were on board when the ship went down? Nobody has seen aught of them, and I worry about them. They're ... friends of mine."

"I know Mary and Anne made it off the ship, Pierre." The expression on his face when she called Mary by her proper name told Abby he knew full well of Mary's charade. When he smiled and winked at her, she also knew he suspected her of some deceptions herself. She simply nodded before continuing. "It's likely they'll be keeping out of sight until it's a bit less ... busy in Port Royal. Don't give up on your friends." She took his hand in hers and gave it a squeeze, and he smiled, unshed tears glistening in his eyes.

"Merci, my dear. I shall look for them when it is bit quieter."

Emelia rapped on the door of the dressing room, and Pierre called, "Enter."

"Ah, I was beginning to think there may be a problem with the gown. Are you ready to go, my dear?" Abby nodded and put her hat on. As she walked to the door, her mother noticed again the ill-fitting shoes she wore, and she turned to Pierre and said, "Do you know of a cobbler that might be able to make some suitable shoes on short notice?"

"This is the wedding of the daughter of the governor, madame. I'm certain something could be done. In fact, I may know just the man. Follow me, please." He led them into the small room that served as his office and scribbled a name and address on a piece of parchment bearing the name of his establishment. "Give this to Robert. I'm certain he will make a fine pair of shoes for your lovely daughter."

Emelia was overjoyed. She very nearly kissed Pierre on the cheek, but instead she took the paper from him and allowed him to kiss the back of her hand. "Merci, monsieur. You are a godsend. I shall ensure the governor sends as much business your way as he possibly can."

"You are too kind, madame. I shall be grateful for his assistance. And please return in the morning … shall we say around ten? I should have the dress ready by then." He turned to Abby, took her hand, and bowed with a most decidedly feminine flourish, before saying, "And to you, ma petite, I wish a most lovely wedding and a life filled with happiness. You shall be the most beautiful bride ever."

Abby blushed furiously as she curtsied. "Thank you, sir. You are most flattering."

Pierre laughed and covered his face with a handkerchief. "Oh my dear, I am no 'sir,' and I intended no flattery, but spoke completely from the heart. Ah, but I'm French, and I have no choice but to speak from the heart, good or bad. And I sense in you perhaps a kindred spirit, no?" He raised his eyebrow and gave her a questioning look. Before she could respond, Emelia took her hand and made for the door.

"Monsieur, I assure you my daughter is not French, and therefore not likely to be kin to you. And we truly must be off as we have so many preparations yet to make and not very much time. I bid you adieu." Abby shrugged her shoulders, but gave Pierre a brief nod and a wink as she was whisked out the door. The sound of the Frenchman's laughter followed them down the street.

The cobbler, Robert, was enough like Pierre to be his brother. He was not much taller than Abby, and his frame was slender as a reed. His voice was soft and almost feminine, and he walked with a mincing gate. But he was most willing to work with the governor's wife and assured her he could make a most lovely pair of shoes if he had until noon the following day. He fitted Abby, his tiny hands soft upon her ankles but quick to complete the task. When Emelia asked what the price would be, he waved her away. He was a Scotsman and knew well the name Hume. "My lady, it is my pleasure to provide these slippers for your beautiful daughter at no charge. 'Tis the least I can do for a Hume. I ask only that you remember me to your friends when they are in need of the best shoes to be had in the Caribbean."

Abby was exhausted by the time her mother was finished dragging her all over Port Royal, where they found a pair of gloves that would work with the gown. Of course the main reason for her exhaustion was the fact that she and Colleen had not slept more than a few hours at a time for the past two nights, and she was simply falling asleep on her feet. When they entered the inn, Abby glanced into the parlor thinking she might find Colleen there. She saw her father deep in conversation with a tall man and realized it was Colleen. Every time she saw her in those dashing clothes, her heart jumped into her throat. Suddenly full of energy, she virtually flew across the room and hooked her arm through Colleen's, a smile wreathing her face.

"Good evening, Abby," Colleen said formally, bowing at her betrothed and kissing the back of her hand before turning toward Emelia and bowing yet again. "Lady Hume, I trust your efforts to secure suitable attire for Abby have been successful."

"Oh, indeed, Captain. The dressmaker promised to have the dress ready first thing in the morning. The cobbler needs a bit more time but said we should have the shoes before midday. Our Abigail will be a vision tomorrow, sir, you may be certain."

"She is a vision now, my lady. I can't keep my eyes off her."

"To be sure, my daughter is a beautiful woman no matter what she wears." She glanced down again at the shoes Colleen had given her to wear and frowned. "Well, there are those shoes. Where on earth did you get them, Abby? And what became of the clothes you were wearing when you were kidnapped?" She bit off the last word as if it left a bitter taste in her mouth.

"Like the dress, these shoes belonged to Charles's sister. Charles was kind enough to let me borrow them. I had to abandon the clothes I wore when we escaped from the ship. It was necessary to disguise myself as a man to get past the guard."

"Good heavens, you dressed as a man? How absurd. You're just a slip of a girl. Why nobody would believe such a thing. It would be as ridiculous as Charles dressing as a woman."

Colleen chuckled. "Yes, indeed, that would be ridiculous."

Abby laughed outright before adding, "I agree, Mother. Charles is simply too tall to be believable as a woman. But he cuts a fine figure of a man."

Shortly after dinner, Emelia retired to her room claiming she felt a headache coming on and hoping to nip it in the bud. Lord Hume also excused himself to take care of some business, leaving Abby and Colleen in the dining room sipping cognac.

"I thought they'd never leave," Abby said after getting up and following her father to make sure he was truly gone. "I love them dearly, but oh, my God, they simply will not leave me alone."

"Ah, but you're their only daughter, and they want what's best for you."

"In their opinion. We have almost never agreed on what 'best' is. But I think I've finally found not only what is best, but what my heart longs for. And since they agree this marriage is a blessing, we actually share an opinion for a change."

Colleen took Abby's hand and kissed the back of her fingers.

"You know we'll have to maintain this sham for the rest of their lives or you may lose favor with them."

"I know, and I'm prepared to do that. But even if somehow they discover the ruse, I would remain with you."

"Even at the cost of your title and estate?"

"The title is a frippery and the estate is a moldering old heap, which is why we came to the Bahamas in the first place. I would gladly go anywhere with you and make my home if it came to that."

"Good to know. For now at least, we will need to live in Scotland where I will be a stranger to the locals. In Hartlepool, they know Charles is dead and at least some people would recognize me. The risk of discovery would be great if your mother and father were to visit."

"Then Scotland it shall be. You'll be introduced as a man, and nobody will question it."

"Let's hope so. And now I fear we should say good night, lest your mother worry about you. From tomorrow, we will not have to sleep separate again." She hooked her arm through Abby's and led her from the room. "I will see you to your door, where I hope to steal one more kiss before we part for the night."

"You need not steal it. I offer kisses freely, but only to you."

The sounds of Abby's mother preparing for bed could be heard through the paper thin walls of the chamber they shared. Not wishing to risk discovery should she open the door, Colleen brought Abby's hand up and lightly brushed her lips across the fingers. "How I wish I could kiss your lips instead," she whispered as she straightened up.

Abby's eyes glistened, and the love she bore for Colleen was apparent in every look and gesture. "Until tomorrow, my captain."

"Yes. Good night, my lady."

That time of year in the Bahamas was usually hotter than the hinges of hell, with humidity that left a body dripping the live long day. June 11 dawned bright, clear, and somewhat cooler, not nearly as oppressive as the usual fare. Colleen was up with the sun, and she asked Mr. Henry to arrange for the bathtub to be brought up from the hold and filled so she might bathe before the wedding. Normally, she made do with a quick cold water wash-up and a splash of French perfume, but today was her wedding day. Wedding day—a day she never thought she would live to see.

Abby wakened to the sounds of her mother puttering around the room, laying out clothes for Abby and herself. Emelia was humming, something she'd not done in years within Abby's hearing. It seemed her mother was as excited about this wedding as Abby was. Almost. The mere thought of what the end of this day would bring gave Abby chills despite the heat. She and Colleen would be married. What she had believed impossible all those months ago when they met was becoming a reality. With a bounce in her step, she bounded to where her mother was busy with her tasks and kissed her on the cheek.

Emelia whirled around and smiled at her daughter, hugging her tightly for a few moments, then releasing her with a tiny shove in the direction of the clothes laid out across her own bed. "Come, dear, we need to be off to the dressmaker's as soon as possible, in case there's a problem with the fitting. Your father will be meeting us in the dining room for supper when we're finished, and you know what a grump he is when kept waiting for a meal." Her tone of voice was lighthearted, belying the words themselves. John Hume was a most soft-spoken and kind man. The last time she heard her husband raise his voice was when their daughter had been kidnapped.

"Oh, pooh, Mother. He would wait all day for the women he loves if he had to. Besides, this is my wedding day—a real wedding this time. I think he knows that time is meaningless right now. We shall arrive when we arrive."

The lilt in Abby's voice made her mother smile and her heart swelled with gladness to see Abby happy at last. And she dared hope that grandchildren still might be in her future. "So we shall. Let me help you into your corset, and please forgive me if I don't do it correctly." As she tightened the laces, she muttered, "How we could have left Nassau without Susan is beyond me."

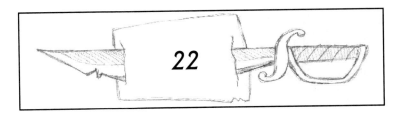

22

"Be still, lass, or I'm liable to lop off your ear," Mr. Henry grumbled as he trimmed Colleen's hair. The quick cut she'd given herself when first she donned her father's clothes was uneven at best, and today was not the day to look unkempt. She stopped squirming and sat still while Mr. Henry finished with a flourish. "There ye go, Col. Not the best haircut but far better than the butchering ye gave yerself." He held up a mirror for her to examine his handiwork, and she had to agree it was a pretty fair cut.

"Not bad, Mr. Henry. I shall make sure my Father takes this into account, as well, when he comes up with your raise." She winked at him as she stood up, brushing the loose hair off her shoulders. "If you'll tie my hair back in a presentable fashion, I'll add to your raise, as well."

"Go on with ye. Not a farthing would I take from yerself." He gathered her hair up in a ponytail and bound it with a scarlet ribbon that matched the coat she would be wearing. She donned the scarlet jacket and wrapped the silk cravat around her neck. He had to smile as she fumbled while trying to tie her cravat. She was probably handier with a knot than anybody on board ship, but it seemed as if she'd grown a second left hand overnight. "Let me give you a hand, Col. Yours don't seem to be functioning all that well today."

"Bless you, Mr. Henry. I do seem to be all thumbs."

When he had a serviceable knot done, he stepped back to survey his handiwork. "You look bonny, lass. Every bit the captain…" His voice trailed off as he thought about her father and wondered how he fared in Andros Town. He shook the thought away; this was Colleen's day, and he did not want to do or say anything to take away from her joy. "As fine looking as your father and that's a fact."

"I wish he could be here to see me get married," she said with a hitch in her voice.

"Aye, I wish so, as well. There is naught but to get this bucket afloat so we can go collect his cantankerous self."

Colleen laughed. "There it is then. I can't wait for him to meet Abby. I know he'll love her." She took her father's three-cornered hat from the peg by the door and set it firmly on her head. She marched to the door, then stopped and turned back to where James stood. "I … I'm not sure if I've told you how much I appreciate what you've done for me. We've never actually talked about … my differences, and I suppose I sort of let you assume what you would. I do hope you don't think less of me for wanting to marry Abby."

"D' ye think I'm daft, lass? I knew from the time you were this high…" He held his hand about waist high on himself. "… that you were a different breed altogether than the other girls. And to tell the truth, it suits you. I'm as proud today as if you were me own daughter, and I am honored you asked me to stand up with you."

"You are like a father to me, Mr. Henry. If my own father cannot be here, there is none but yourself I want by my side."

"Then you need to get aboard the *Gypsy Queen* and I'll follow with the *Betsy Ann* as planned. When you are in international waters and drop anchor, I'll be in the jolly boat before you come to a complete stop."

The *Gypsy Queen* was festooned with streamers and flowers that swayed with the freshening breeze. Colleen didn't know whether it was Abby's idea or her mother's, but she had to admit the schooner looked festive and gay. She walked up the gangplank with her head high and her heart thumping so loudly she thought they could hear it below decks. One of the sailors who was working the sails directed her aft to where the governor and his wife were discussing arrangements with the captain of the ship. She thanked him and made her way to where they were engrossed in conversation. She cleared her throat to get their attention, and Lady Hume looked up to see her standing there.

"Captain Edwards, please join us. Captain Thompson, this is Captain Edwards, soon to be my son-in-law."

The two shook hands, and Captain Thompson furrowed his brow as if in thought. "You look familiar to me, Captain, yet I'm certain we've not met."

Colleen realized she'd met him perhaps three years earlier when the *Betsy Ann* was part of a convoy of ships escorting the king around the British Isles. The *Gypsy Queen* was part of the same convoy, and the captains obviously knew each other. "You met my father, sir. He was … is the captain of the *Betsy Ann*. I'm merely standing in until he can resume his duties." She only hoped Captain Thompson did not look too closely at her, as he'd flirted with her most unashamedly, and she had rebuffed him as she always did. As she remembered it, he did not take her rejection very well. Colleen wished she'd remembered why the name of this vessel seemed familiar to her. She might have suggested they try to find another way to get married. There was nothing to it but to go forward, so she put on a brave face and even smiled at the little worm.

"Of course, that's it. Those eyes are just the same as his. But I don't remember him having a son. He had a daughter, as I recall, a beautiful girl." He twirled his mustache and smiled as he visualized the lovely young woman who unfortunately wished to have nothing to do with him. Her loss, he mused.

Thinking fast, Colleen said, "I was serving in the Royal Navy at the time, Captain. My sister sailed with our father after the death of our mother, and she is even now tending to him due to a wound he received while attempting to rescue Miss Hume. The *Betsy Ann* will be returning for him immediately upon completion of the wedding, so I request we get underway with all speed."

"We're nearly ready, Captain. I didn't realize there was another reason for your desire for an immediate wedding beyond the obvious." He winked at her as if to say he knew the young captain had compromised the lady, and the governor insisted they be married.

Not wanting to remain in his presence any longer than absolutely necessary, Colleen turned toward Emelia. "Lady Hume, would it be possible for me to see Abby?"

"Oh, Captain, it would be bad luck for you to see her before the wedding." Her tone was light, but her face was entirely serious.

Not wishing to upset her future mother-in-law, Colleen sighed and said, "Well then, I'll go and see if I might assist the lads in getting us cast off. If you'll excuse me." She turned to go, but Emelia clutched her arm and held fast.

"Please stay and talk with us, Charles. We have only a few hours to get to know you before you take our daughter away from us. We want to know all about you—your family, where you're from, oh, everything." Emelia took two glasses of wine from a tray carried by a sailor and handed one to Colleen.

"I'm from Hartlepool, on the north coast of England, the oldest of three children. My youngest brother and mother died in a cholera epidemic in 1709." Emelia patted Colleen's hand, her face sympathetic and rapt as Colleen continued to tell the partially true story of her past, embellished with the fictional exploits of Charles in the Royal Navy. She neglected to mention having met Abby before the day of her kidnapping. She ended her tale with the rescue itself, playing down her part in it and lauding Abby for her bravery during the ordeal. "I confess I was smitten with her from the moment I laid eyes on her."

Emelia smiled at her. "She is a lovely girl. It's easy to see how you could be captivated by her. Many other men have made the same claim of devotion, but she spurned them all. I'm simply delighted she's finally decided to settle down—and with such a fine figure of a man as yourself."

Colleen was taking a sip of wine and nearly choked when Emelia finished speaking. Coughing and catching her breath, she said, "I'm the lucky one indeed to have captured such a precious heart as Abby's. I intend to spend the rest of my life working to make her happy."

"Abby said you plan to live in Scotland. I'm so pleased. When John's appointment here is complete, we hope to return home and find a whole raft of grandchildren to spoil."

Colleen smiled. "If it is meant to be, my lady," she said with a bow.

The ship's bell sounded to let them know they were beyond the limits of Port Royal and within international waters. Colleen spent the time between their departure and arrival at this point alternating between pacing about the deck and checking to see that the *Betsy Ann* was keeping them in sight. When the bell sounded, Colleen took a lantern and stood at the railing, waving it until she saw the light from the *Betsy Ann* winking back at her. She smiled to think that Mr. Henry would be with her soon. Her isolation from Abby left her feeling lonely for the familiar, and at that moment, he was the closest to a father she had.

Captain Thompson emerged from his cabin and very nearly ran into Colleen as she stood at the rail. "Oh, beg pardon, Captain Edwards. I didn't see you there."

He had changed into his dress uniform, and Colleen had to admit he was not a bad-looking man. If only he was not such a sniveling snake. "No harm done, Captain. Are we ready to proceed with the ceremony?" The splash of the anchor hitting the water was her answer.

"As soon as your best man arrives, we'll start."

"Ahoy, *Gypsy Queen*! James Henry requesting permission to come aboard!"

True to his word, as soon as the *Gypsy Queen* lowered her sails, Mr. Henry brought the *Betsy Ann* as close as he could safely get to the other vessel, and the jolly boat was lowered to the water. He was wearing his very best uniform, complete with the sword his father had given him. The last time Colleen remembered seeing him wear it was at the funeral for her family. Colleen blinked back the tears that pooled in her eyes and made her way to the rope ladder. She held out her hand and helped the old sailor climb aboard.

"Good to see you again, Mr. Henry," she said, clapping him on the back.

"And you, as well, Captain. Sorry me old uniform don't fit so good anymore, but it's the best I could do on short notice." The coat was more than a little tight on him and the fabric thin in spots, but to her eyes, he looked quite dapper.

"You look perfect," Colleen said with a huge grin. "I'm so glad to have you here. Come, the sooner we get this done, the sooner we can get out of these monkey suits."

Captain Thompson and Emelia were waiting on deck by the mainmast, and those crewmen not engaged in ship's duties stood around to observe the proceedings. As Colleen and Mr. Henry approached, the captain gave a nod to one of the crewmen who held a small accordion in front of his chest. The man began to play a slow march, and all assembled turned toward the quarterdeck, where Abby stood beside her father.

Colleen could not imagine anything more beautiful than Abby wearing the dress her mother made, but clearly her imagination was not what it should be. The woman standing at the top of the stairs was so beautiful, looking at her took Colleen's breath away. The dress she wore was cream-colored with tiny pearl buttons on the sleeves. Around the neck was a delicate lace, and the same lace surrounded Abby's wrists. Her hair was gathered by a blue ribbon, and the blond curls cascaded down to her shoulders. Surprisingly, the shoes were a match to the color of the dress, and it appeared as if the entire ensemble had been planned for months in advance instead of merely one day. Colleen could feel her eyes beginning to fill with tears, and she gulped a large breath of air and shook her head to clear the mist away.

Side by side, they came down the stairs, both wearing smiles so wide it was impossible to determine who was the happier.

The governor walked Abby to where Colleen stood beside Mr. Henry, and after kissing her cheek, he gave her hand to Colleen and stepped back.

Colleen turned to look into Abby's face, and the love she felt for her bloomed anew in her breast. Her eyes brimmed with tears once again, and she brushed them away with her free hand.

Abby smiled at Colleen, sending her a silent message of strength and love with the look and the pressure of her hand. Together they turned toward Captain Thompson, who cleared his throat and began.

"As duly appointed captain of this vessel, it is within my authority to join a man and a woman in wedlock. Charles Edwards the second and Abigail Hume stand before me for this purpose. Who gives this woman to be married?"

"I do," John Hume replied, his voice gravelly with emotion.

"And who will stand up for this man?"

"I will," answered Mr. Henry without hesitation. He stepped up beside Colleen and gave her a huge grin.

"Do you have vows prepared that you wish to share with the people here assembled before I pronounce you man and wife?"

Colleen realized she'd not given any thought to what might be expected of her during the ceremony. She looked at Abby, cleared her throat, and said, "Abby, you have made me the happiest person on earth today. I promise I will spend my life loving and caring for you until there is no more breath in my body. And even unto eternity, I will stand by you and treasure you always for the gift you are to me. I love you with all my heart and soul. You complete me and fill my heart with love and gladness."

Abby's eyes overflowed with the tears she could no longer contain. She took Colleen's hands, looked into her face, and said, "I vow to love you all the days of my life and beyond. You make me whole and happy, and I want nothing more than to do the same for you. I will support you in all your endeavors and hold you up when you stumble. I adore you—and I always will."

Captain Thompson cleared his throat again. "Marriage is a sacred institution and one which must not be entered into lightly. Charles, you have promised to love Abigail all the days of your life. I ask that you reaffirm you will provide for her and cherish her so long as you both shall live, whether in hardship or plenty, sickness or health. Do you make this promise now before these witnesses?"

"With all my heart, I do," Colleen said.

"Abigail, a wife must be the backbone of her family with the strength and courage to overcome adversity in lockstep with her husband. She must run his household and bear his children all with grace and dignity as befits his station. She must honor and obey him and not give him cause to punish her—"

Colleen held up her hand to stop him, and he looked at her curiously. "Captain Thompson, ours will be an equal partnership. I shall not ask that Abby obey me because we will make decisions together. And I would never raise my hand to punish her, nor shall my words become so sharp as to wound her. I cannot ask her to agree to that last line, sir."

Abby smiled at Colleen, then turned toward the captain, who stared at Colleen with a most perplexed expression on his face. "Captain Thompson, I agree with Charles. The word 'obey' should be stricken from the marriage ceremony if two people are truly partners. As long as we are in agreement on this point, may we continue without that word?"

"I … I suppose there's nothing to prevent it, but it is most odd indeed." He shook his head as if to indicate he washed his hands of the entire affair. "Well then, where was I … oh, yes, I trust that you do not object to the word 'honor'?" He waited until Abby and Colleen both nodded their affirmation, then continued. "Abigail, will you honor and cherish Charles for as long as you both shall live, whether in hardship or plenty, sickness or health? Do you make this promise now before these witnesses?"

"I do."

"Do you have rings to exchange?" Captain Thompson was well aware the wedding had been thrown together with very little planning and doubted there would be any rings available. He was surprised when Mr. Henry stepped up beside Colleen. He reached into his pocket and brought out a small box, which he handed to her.

"I have, sir," Colleen said as she removed the gold band from the box. She took Abby's left hand in her own and waited for the captain to continue.

"Repeat after me. I pledge my troth to thee."

"I pledge my troth to thee," Colleen echoed as she raised the ring before Abby's finger.

"My commitment to you has no beginning and no end, as it is with this gold band."

"My commitment to you has no beginning and no end, as it is with this gold band."

"With this ring, I thee wed."

"With this ring, I thee wed." She slid the ring onto Abby's finger.

Lord Hume stepped forward and whispered into Abby's ear. She smiled as he removed a signet ring from his little finger and handed it to her. Her hand trembled as she reached for Colleen's hand and paused with the ring ready to put on her finger. At Captain Thompson's direction, Abby repeated the same words as Colleen had before her.

"On the eleventh day of June in the year of our Lord 1717, with the power vested in me as captain of His Majesty's vessel *Gypsy Queen*, I pronounce you husband and wife. You may kiss the bride."

Colleen leaned down and placed a gentle kiss on Abby's lips. The strangeness of kissing her in the company of others was quickly overcome. She could get used to being able to show affection to the woman she loved and not worry about being shunned. With hands joined, they turned to face the people assembled on deck, both of their faces full of the joy and love they could not hide even if they wanted to.

"I give you ... Captain and Mrs. Charles Edwards the second." Emelia sobbed openly as the couple approached, and she gathered Abby into her arms when she was within reach.

"Och, lass, how wonderful it is to see you look so happy. I'm glad you turned down the suitors who called on you since Arthur's death. One does not need eyes to see that you two are meant to be together."

"Thank you, Mother. I think so, too." She kissed her mother's cheek, then moved to where her father stood, flinging her arms around his shoulders. "Oh, Father, thank you for the ring. With all that was going on yesterday, I completely forgot about a ring."

"I should have thought of it earlier myself. That ring will

show all who meet him that he's part of the Hume clan and due all the respect a Hume demands."

He puffed out his chest a bit but deflated somewhat when Abby replied, "If he's due respect, it's because he's a good and honest man, not because of the family he married into. He does not demand respect, it is given to him freely. That is one of the many things I love about him, Father. I hope you will feel the same once you get to know him."

"He saved your life. That alone earned my respect. How he obviously loves you ensures my loyalty to him. Bless you both. I wish you all the happiness you deserve."

Colleen could not help but hear the exchange between Abby and her father, but she remained where she stood until Abby reached out to draw her near.

Lord Hume grasped Colleen's hand in his and gave it a firm shake. "I'm proud to call you son, Charles. I can never repay the debt I owe you for what you've done, but I plan to keep trying. For a start, our home and holdings are yours to command."

"Thank you, my lord. I'm honored to be part of your family and hope you never have reason to believe you have misplaced your trust in me." Mr. Henry tapped Colleen on the shoulder and indicated with a nod that he'd like a word with her. They stepped out of earshot and conversed for a few moments, after which Colleen returned to her place by Abby's side and once again took hold of her hand. "The wind is getting up, your lordship. Unfortunately, we need to be underway soon to take advantage of it. If my father is fit to travel, I promise we will stop at Nassau before we journey to Scotland."

"Godspeed, both of you. I pray your father is well on the road to recovery and hope we shall see you all in the near future." He drew Abby into his arms for one more hug, reluctantly letting go only when Emelia reached out for her.

Abby could not hold back the tears when her mother began sobbing as she clutched her close. "I love you, Mother. Please don't cry, I beg you, or you'll have me crying all of my wedding night."

"I don't know why I'm crying, dear. I'm beyond happy right

now. I'm just not sure how I'll face that big house without your cheerful face and lilting laughter to brighten it up. Oh, Abby, how I'll miss you. Now I only wish for your father's appointment as governor to end so we can return to Scotland to see you."

Colleen took Lady Hume's hand and kissed it, bowing deeply to her. She was surprised when the lady pulled her close and gave her a hug.

"You take good care of our girl," she admonished as she released Colleen.

"Be assured, my lady, I will care for her as if she were the Crown Jewels."

Colleen led Abby to the railing and said, "Wait here a moment while I climb down, Abby. Mr. Henry will lower you into my arms. Are you ready?" Mr. Henry had already arranged for Abby's few possessions to be lowered to the jolly boat, so there was nothing left but the three of them. Colleen waved at her new father-in-law and mother-in-law as she disappeared over the side. Abby blew them kisses when Mr. Henry picked her up and gingerly lowered her to Colleen's waiting arms.

Mr. Henry assured Colleen that he didn't mind handling the ship until they dropped anchor for the night, and he practically pushed her toward her father's cabin. "'Tis not every day you get married, Captain. Go and be with your lovely bride. The seas are calm, and there's nothing so important ye can't wait till tomorrow to deal with it." When she hesitated, Mr. Henry scowled at her and wagged his finger. "Go along with ye." He put his hands on her shoulders and gave her a small push in the direction of the captain's cabin. She shrugged and did as he asked. If he wanted to handle the ship without her, who was she to argue?

Abby was already in the cabin wearing her night dress. Before going topside to talk with Mr. Henry, Colleen had helped her remove the gown and petticoats and neatly fold them into her own trunk. Once Colleen knew for certain she was not needed on deck, she could relax and allow Abby to help her out of her uniform and the bindings that held her breasts. She would be happy when her father was once again in command of the vessel, and she no longer needed to hide her gender on board. Once they arrived in Scotland, the story would be different, but for now, she just wanted to be herself. She sighed and stretched, loving the freedom of motion gained by the removal of the bindings.

Abby drank in the form of her husband as the skin was revealed. "I'll never tire of looking at you, my love. I wish I could paint you—just like that—but sadly I would not be able to share the painting with another soul but you."

"Paint me with your mind, then you can call up my image whenever you wish without fear of discovery."

"Och, I have painted you with my mind since the day we met. I have an entire museum of images stored up there." She tapped her head with a finger, an impish smile on her face. "Now I wish to paint you with my hands and mouth. Would that be all right with you, husband?"

"Most certainly, my dear wife, provided I am allowed the same privilege. It is our wedding day, after all."

"That seems fair." Abby pulled her nightgown over her head and walked to the chair at the foot of the bed, where she folded and laid it down neatly. Naked, she turned to where Colleen stood. "Now please bring your luscious body over here so I may touch you," Abby said. Her voice was low, almost a growl.

Colleen could feel herself getting wet just at the sound of Abby's voice. She hastened to the side of the bunk where Abby stood. When she was so close there was scarcely room for a piece of parchment between them, she asked, "Am I close enough, love?"

Abby's hands moved first to Colleen's breasts, and after squeezing them until Colleen closed her eyes and began to moan, she let them travel down her abdomen, then around her back where she cupped her cheeks and pulled her even closer. "Now you are."

Abby buried her fingers in Colleen's thick black hair and pulled her head down so their lips met. The kiss was soft at first, almost tentative, but when Colleen responded by parting her lips and touching her tongue to Abby's mouth, they became almost frantic in their need to touch deeply.

Colleen explored Abby's mouth with her tongue, then

withdrew to trace the contours of her lips.

"Oh, Colleen," Abby said when they separated. "You take my breath away, lass."

"You do the same to me. 'Tis a wonder we're able to stand." She cupped Abby's head in her hands and ran her thumbs lightly over her brows, cheekbones, and lips.

Abby sighed again and closed her eyes. When she opened them, Colleen was staring at her with equal parts of love and desire. "For safety's sake then, let's lie down. I fear my legs will not continue to hold me up much longer."

Colleen laughed, but she sat on the edge of the bed and drew Abby down until she was straddling her legs, the moisture of her desire pressing hotly against her. Abby's breasts were within reach of Colleen's eager mouth, and she took full advantage of her position by gathering first one breast, then the other to be feasted on. Abby assisted her efforts by thrusting her chest toward her waiting mouth. When Abby groaned, Colleen placed her hand over her mouth and whispered, "Abby, we aren't alone on board anymore. Do you want every man on board to know what we're doing?"

"I don't give a bloody damn what they know. It's our wedding day. I think we're supposed to make noise."

Colleen laughed again, delighted at Abby's response. "Very well, my lady. Prepare to make more noise." She descended once again on Abby's breasts, while her hand wandered to the damp valley between her legs.

And Abby made a lot more noise.

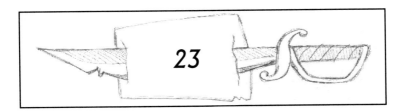

23

Upon arrival in Andros Town, Colleen went straight to the home of the doctor. She was surprised to find him not only alive, but also quite eager to be out of the confinement of his sick bed. His eyes widened as he took in the look of his daughter in his finest uniform and with a lovely blonde on her arm. Charles dismissed the doctor from his sickroom with a promise to not exert himself, and the doctor left, but not without looking Colleen up and down as if trying to place her.

"Father, I was so worried I would return to find you had not survived, and here you are, ordering the doctor around in his own home."

"He's a fussbudget, and I wanted to be able to speak with you freely. I see you've assumed command of the *Betsy Ann*. How did you manage to get the crew to obey your orders?"

"Ah, well—I asked Mr. Henry to get me a new crew, one who would not know I was not a man. He found some good lads. And there is one man I'd like to keep on. With your permission, of course," she hastened to add.

"I trust your judgment, Col." He shifted his gaze to Abby and flashed a big smile. "Do I have the honor of addressing the daughter of the governor?"

Abby curtsied and said, "You do, sir, but the honor is mine. I have so wanted to meet the man who raised this most brave and beautiful woman." She reached out for Colleen's hand and twined their fingers together.

"Her mother had that pleasure. I simply allowed her to bully me into taking her to sea." He laughed, then flinched when a sharp pain stabbed his side. "Ouch. Please remind me not to laugh, it hurts."

"I'm sure you played a large part in shaping the magnificent creature she is."

Colleen was embarrassed at the attention. Her cheeks were flushed a most charming pink, and she cast her eyes toward the floor. "Abby, please—I'm nothing special."

"Ha! Nothing special she says." She approached Charles's bed and he patted the edge to indicate she should sit. She dropped down beside him and began to talk as if she'd known him all her life. She told him about the nightmare of being held captive and not knowing whether her father would be able to get the ransom together in time to save her. But mostly, she talked about Colleen, how she rigged the ship to blow up, taking many of the pirates with it to Davy Jones's locker. "And when my father arrived, Colleen asked him for my hand in marriage. He said yes." She held up her hand to show him the ring she wore. "Show him your ring, Colleen." She held out her hand, and Colleen came closer, placing her left hand in Abby's. Charles looked at their two hands together, the rings sparkling like sunlight on the ocean. "Colleen told me she was sure you would approve of our marriage."

"Colleen revealed to me how she felt about you the same day you were kidnapped. I told her then, and I say it again now, her happiness is all I care about. And it's clear she is happier now than I have seen in her adult life." He took Colleen's hand and looked closely at the ring, noting the crest of the Hume clan. "I'm proud of you for your ingenuity in rescuing her and for your honesty in coming to me to tell me of your plans."

"Father, you're my only family. I could not imagine leaving you out of my life, for that is surely what I would have had to do if I'd not told you. And because I fear the people in Hartlepool would not accept me and Abby as a couple, we have decided to make our home in Scotland, where I can continue to appear as a man while in public."

Charles's face went slack as he listened to his daughter talk about living so far away from their family home. He was not sure how many more years he could continue to captain the *Betsy Ann* and hoped Colleen would agree to take over when he stepped down. Abby saw the look in his eyes and guessed at the source of his discomfort.

"Sir, please know that you are welcome to live with us in Edinburgh. And Colleen has told me she plans to continue sailing with you as long as you need her."

Charles grasped Abby's hand and kissed her fingers gently. "You are indeed a treasure, Abby. I'm so happy for you ... for both of you."

Abby leaned down to kiss Charles's forehead, a tear quietly sliding down her cheek

"My father will be resuming his duties as captain of the *Betsy Ann* when we set sail, lads." Before departing for the doctor's house, Colleen had asked the crew to meet her the following day at the local tavern to discuss what her next steps would be. "For your help in making sure we reached Port Royal in time to rescue the governor's daughter, I wanted to thank each of you personally and to give you a bonus as my thanks." She handed each man two doubloons, then waved to the bartender. "Drinks on me for these lads, my good man."

When all of the men crowded up to the bar, Colleen motioned for one to join her at a small table. As soon as he had settled with a tankard of ale in front of him, Colleen said, "Tom, I would like you to consider continuing on with me. I know it's short notice, and you—"

"Aye, Cap'n! It would be an honor to serve with you."

"I don't mean just on the ship, but when we arrive in Scotland, as well. If it doesn't suit you there and you wish to return to England after a time, I'll understand. I couldn't bear the thought of leaving you here since it seemed it was not your choice to begin with."

"You've been kinder to me than anybody I know," Tom said. "Even the night you thumped me on the head. I would gladly stay with you and happily do any task you wish."

Tom was the young crewman from the *William* whose clothes Colleen borrowed. When she sent Mr. Henry to untie him and offer the lad work aboard the *Betsy Anne*, he quickly agreed. It seemed Mr. Dell, the first mate on board the *William*, had taken a fancy to Tom when the lad was working as an apprentice to a baker in South Hampton. He promised him a boatswain's job on the ship and hinted at treasures and riches rivaling anything the young man could hope for as a baker. Tom, who was a bit simple, believed the promises and signed on to depart the following day. Instead of being a boatswain, he was put to work as a powder monkey. He toiled until his fingers bled and saw more than one other powder monkey blown to pieces by incoming cannon balls. And most nights, Mr. Dell ordered him to come to his cabin, where he would satisfy his somewhat twisted sexual cravings on him. The chance at a new and better life was more than welcome.

The crew of the *Betsy Ann* languished a fortnight in Andros Town while Charles built up his strength, then set sail for Nassau.

Colleen trod softly across the wooden planks lest the sound of the creaking timbers waken her sleeping wife. Abby was suffering from a headache and had slept only a few hours the night before. Colleen sat on a stool near the bed and watched the even rise and fall of Abby's breast. She had to stop from time to time to remind herself they really were together and no longer had to steal an hour here and there when Colleen was in port. Abby rolled her head toward where Colleen sat, and a sigh escaped her lips. Colleen reached out and brushed the hair from Abby's forehead, marveling at the silken softness of it. Abby's eyes slowly opened to find Colleen sitting there wearing her father's best uniform again.

"I do love you in that uniform, Col. What a dashing figure you cut."

Colleen laughed. "Ah, so it's the clothes you fell for then? And here I thought it was my body you loved."

"Och, it is your body, as well as your kindness and gentle ways, also for your bravery and determination. But you do cut quite the figure in that impressive uniform, my love." Abby winked and laughed and reached up to pull Colleen down for a kiss. Their lips met in a gentle kiss that heated up when Abby twined her fingers into Colleen's hair and pulled her even closer.

Colleen moaned when Abby's tongue slid between her lips, and it was all she could do to push herself away from the unspoken invitation. "Oh, Abby, how I would love to crawl in there with you and make love all day."

"Then why don't you? My headache is gone, and I'm full of energy." She wiggled her eyebrows to show her forehead was free from the creases that marked it the night before.

"Temptress," Colleen said with a laugh. "But I can't because we're no more than an hour out from Nassau, and you still need to dress so we can visit your mother and father. Unless you'd rather not...."

"Och, you know I miss them and can't wait to see them. Why didn't you tell me we were so close?" She sprang out of bed and began to peel off her nightgown. She'd never spent a night without them near before she was captured by pirates. Her heart ached with missing them while she was on Rackham's ship, but truth be told, the thought she might never see Colleen again was what made her cry herself to sleep every night. Abby rummaged through the trunk at the foot of the bed, tossing items in all directions. Colleen purchased two dresses for her in Andros Town—one for everyday wear and the other a plaid dress with the Hume tartan. The wedding gown and the dress Colleen gave her were both far too dressy to wear all the time. "Where is the plaid one? Mother will be envious of it, I know."

"Stop tossing things about, Abby," Colleen said, shaking her head and laughing. "I put it in the wardrobe to keep it from wrinkling. I knew you'd want to wear it for your family." She reached into the wardrobe and pulled out the dress. "Now if you can settle down for just a bit, I'll help you into your corset and petticoats."

"I'd rather you help me off with my clothes than on," Abby said. "But I guess there's no time—now. Just you remember where we left off when we get back here later on, my love."

The timbre of Abby's voice sent a jolt straight to Colleen's center, and she nodded enthusiastically. "You can be certain of it."

Colleen felt as if she were dreaming as she sat in the parlor of the governor's house, a cup of tea in her hand, Abby sitting on one side of her and her father on the other. Lord John and Lady Emelia were on the settee across from Colleen, their faces wreathed in smiles. She could almost picture Emelia's face when the servant informed her Charles Edwards—Senior and Junior—and Mrs. Charles Edwards were calling. They waited no more than five minutes before Emelia bustled into the room, followed closely by John. Colleen recalled the moment, and it made her smile.

"Abigail, you look positively radiant," Emelia had gushed at first sight of her daughter. "Och, that dress is beautiful. I must have one just like it." She turned to Colleen and held out her hand, which Colleen accepted, placing a kiss on the knuckles. "Charles, you have breathed life into our daughter. She was a pale flower before you met her, and now she's a dazzling bouquet of color. As long as I live, I will be grateful to you for what you've done for our little girl."

"I was honor bound to do what I could to assist, my lady. That I fell in love with Abby and she agreed to marry me was a most happy twist of fate." It was not prudent to say she'd fallen in love with Abby long before the abduction and would have sacrificed her own life gladly if required to save the beautiful woman now sitting beside her.

Emelia turned her attention to Charles and once again held out her hand for the obligatory kiss. Charles brushed his lips across her knuckles before bestowing a smile upon her. "We're so relieved you survived the wound you sustained at the hands of that horrible pirate. It's heartening to know you instilled the values in your son that made him carry on in your place, when I'm certain he wanted nothing more than to stay with you to ensure you were well. And I'm truly glad we were able to meet before you returned to England."

"My lady, it's an honor to meet you both. It was ... er ... Charles' quick action that kept me alive so we could be here today to celebrate the marriage of our children. But believe me, the values my ... son ... has are courtesy of his sainted mother and through no effort of my own." Concerned that he might use the wrong name or pronoun, Charles simply shrugged and stopped speaking.

Colleen could tell her father was having difficulty participating in a conversation fraught with pitfalls that might result in exposing her charade. "Don't believe him," she said with a note of pride in her voice. "He's the best father anyone could have and has taught me by example about honor and valor. I am who I am because of him."

"Well, of course you are. I can tell your father is modest. And both of you are most heartily welcomed into our family. Please, let us retire to the parlor where we can have some tea and scotch scones, made from an old family recipe. If I'd known you were going to be here today, we would have prepared something a bit more elegant."

Two hours passed and the scones were gone. The dregs of the tea were now tepid in the pot, yet all of them seemed to be reluctant for the visit to end. But evening would soon give way to night, and the walk to the port in the dark was not something Colleen wanted to subject Abby to. As if reading her mind, Abby rose from the sofa and crossed to where her mother sat. She leaned down and kissed her on the cheek and said, "We need to say good night, Mother. Charles and I will be back in the morning to pack my things and hope you both have time to visit with us. I realize this is unexpected—"

"Oh, darling, I have nothing to do that could possibly be more important than spending more time with you. Your father can cancel any appointments he may have, I think." She looked at John, who nodded his assent. "You must come as early as you can and have tea with us. Stay all day, if you're able."

Abby turned to Colleen with a pleading look on her face and said, "Is it all right, dear? I mean, might we spend the entire day here?" Abby had taken to calling Colleen dear while they were en route to Nassau so that she wouldn't slip and call her by her name. Colleen smiled at the endearment, so it seemed like the right thing to do.

"I need to oversee the loading of some cargo we left here before setting out for Port Royal. Once I'm certain all is under control, I'm yours for the day." Colleen rose and took Emelia's hand to kiss her fingers once again. It amazed her how easily she fell into the habits of men, and she was grateful she was able to pull it off convincingly. She hated to think what would happen if her in-laws were to discover her ruse.

"Abby and I will amuse ourselves until you join us then," Emelia said as she hooked her arm through her daughter's and pulled her close.

Charles stood up, walked to where Lord Hume sat, and held out his hand. The governor got to his feet, as well, shaking hands firmly with Charles. "Lord Hume, thank you for your hospitality. I only wish we could stay in Nassau a bit longer, but our cargo is already a month late, and I fear we'll have an angry client on our hands if we delay further. I promise my son and I will take good care of Abby, who is already firmly entrenched in my heart as well as his."

"That is our only consolation in losing our daughter, sir. I can tell you both care deeply for her, and it's a great weight off my mind. Will we see you again tomorrow, Captain?"

"No, my lord. I must catch up on a mountain of paperwork, and resting at anchor is the best time to do it. I bid you both a good evening and hope to see you again upon future visits to your sunny shores."

Colleen stretched out on her father's bunk, her long legs reflecting ghostly white in the flicker of the lamp light. She was grateful to her father for allowing her to continue the use of his cabin since her own small space scarcely accommodated herself and would certainly make for cramped quarters with Abby on board. She glanced down to where Abby lay with her head pillowed on her breast, her breathing soft and even in sleep. After dealing with the mundane chores of securing the ship, the two had retired to the cabin, where true to her word, Abby reminded her of where they left off before going ashore, and they made love until they were both unable to move. Placing a kiss on Abby's forehead, Colleen allowed herself to drift to sleep.

Abby stretched and groaned, her muscles vigorously protesting the most strenuous workout they were just subjected to. Her hand rested on Colleen's breast, and without consciously willing it, she pinched Colleen's nipple, feeling it harden under her hand. Abby had never before in her life slept without a gown, and to be able to feel Colleen's naked form against her own nakedness was a constant source of excitement. Just when she thought she could not take another moment of lovemaking, her hand would encounter Colleen's soft breast or smooth thigh, and her heart would leap at the thought of making love to her again. "Are you asleep, dear?" she asked softly. She knew Colleen had a great deal of work to do in the morning before she could join her in the governor's mansion, and she really needed to let her sleep. But that enticing breast was calling her name; she could swear she heard it.

"Not anymore," Colleen said, chuckling. "How you can wake up from a dead sleep after making love for hours and still have the energy to fondle so much as a nipple is beyond me."

"It's not my fault," Abby pouted. "If I'd known how wonderful you could make me feel when we first met, I'd have seduced you and carried you away somewhere."

"And your father would have chased us down and hanged me. I think it was much better that we waited. Now we have the freedom to make love as much as we like, and nobody can stop us."

"Well, yes, that's true. I guess I should stop lamenting what we missed and celebrate what we have. I do love you so, Colleen."

"Oh, Abby, there is nothing on this earth I love more than you, and I'll spend the rest of my life showing you just how much.

Starting right now." She rose up on her elbow and shifted so Abby was lying beneath her. Kissing her way from her lips to her neck, then to her breasts, she dragged her tongue over Abby's hardening nipple, feeling the skin around it contract.

It would be two hours later before the newlyweds slept again.

Two days later, the cargo and Abby's trunks loaded in the hold, Colleen and Abby stood on the dock, bidding Emelia and John farewell.

Emelia clung to Abby, tears brimming in her eyes, which she resolutely forbade to fall. She always knew when Abby finally married she would lose her, and she was resigned to it. But she harbored a hope Abby would marry someone local so they would still be able to see each other. It would be at least two years before she and John returned to Scotland, and that seemed like a lifetime to her. "Now you promised to write at least once a week. Charles, you see that she does, won't you?"

Colleen nodded. "Yes of course, my lady. And if ever she is not up to writing, I'll write to you myself. You'll have all the news of home, I promise."

"Oh, thank you, dear. You're such a treasure." Emelia patted Colleen's hand. "I don't know if I said it before, but you two make the most beautiful couple I've ever seen. I just know your babies will be beautiful, as well."

"Mother, please. If babies are in our future, I'm sure they'll be the most beautiful in your eyes, even if they are ugly little beasts. But please don't be disappointed if we don't have any. Not every woman is made to bear children." Emelia made no secret over the years that she yearned for grandchildren, and Abby wanted to prepare her now that there would be no offspring forthcoming.

"Leave me my dreams, dear, will you? I hope to find a houseful of babies when we return to Scotland in two years."

"As you wish." She hugged her mother, and Emelia could not hold back a sob. "Please don't cry, Mother. Be happy for me."

"I am, my precious. I'll simply miss you every moment until we see you again, that's all."

Charles came striding down the gangplank and joined the group, greeting John and Emelia formally before turning to Colleen. "We need to get underway soon. The wind is up."

"I know, Father. We were just coming." She turned to her in-laws with a smile. "Lady Emelia, I bid you farewell. You have my most sincere thanks for raising such a wonderful woman as Abby." Grasping John's hand, she gave it a hearty shake and said, "And to you, sir, my thanks for allowing me to marry her. I'm grateful beyond my ability to express it. She will be treasured and taken care of for the rest of her life, you may be sure."

Abby hugged each of her parents once again before twining her fingers through Colleen's and walking toward the gangplank.

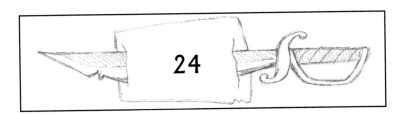

24

Abby wept when the *Betsy Ann* pulled into the port of Leith, north of Edinburgh. Nearly two years had passed since she left home, but until she saw the stone buildings that were the hallmark of Scottish architecture, she hadn't realized how much she missed it.

Colleen put her arm around Abby's waist and pulled her close. She leaned down and placed a kiss on Abby's cheek, noting the salty tears that coated her lips. "Sorry if this is a sad homecoming, my love," she whispered.

Abby snuggled closer to her and looked up with a smile on her face. "Not sad, Col. It's … strange to be here without Mother and Father, and perhaps being so close to home reminds me they're not here. But sad? Never, not with you by my side."

"By your side I will be for the rest of my life. And I look forward to seeing your home. You have described it so well, I feel like I know each stone already."

"Our home," Abby corrected. "I was afraid I was boring you with all the stories about the place. It's in quite a state of disrepair, but it's home."

"I believe you called it a moldering old heap before," Colleen said, laughing. "A state of disrepair does not sound so bad. Come, let's collect our things and be off so I can see it through my own eyes. Ah, here's Tom now."

Tom came up behind them, dragging a chest that seemed to be larger than he was. "Here's the last of them, Cap," he said, straightening up and stretching out his aching muscles. During the long ocean voyage, Tom and Colleen became rather good friends, and the lad decided he would like to stay on with her in Scotland rather than returning to England. He was a hard worker, even if it was sometimes necessary to explain things to him more than once. He also confessed to Colleen that even before Mr. Dell soiled him, he found men more appealing than women. Colleen made him feel like it was acceptable to be attracted to his own gender, so when she offered him a job on the estate in Scotland, he agreed immediately. Since the death of his mother, there was nobody in England who treated him as kindly as Colleen did, and he was glad to have her call him friend.

"Thank you, Tom. Would you please go and see about having a large wagon brought 'round to carry our luggage?"

"Aye, Cap. I'll be back in a trice." He set off down the gangplank at a run.

Colleen smiled and shook her head as she watched him go. Her brother Thomas would have been about the same age as this lad, and perhaps that was part of the reason she felt so drawn to him. It seemed right somehow to do what she could to take care of him, especially since he'd been treated cruelly at the hands of Mr. Dell. "He'll break a leg one day if he keeps that up," she muttered under her breath.

"He adores you, you know," Abby said as she watched the young man disappear behind a warehouse. "It was very kind of you to let him stay on with you." She also had a fondness for Tom and probably would have suggested he stay with them if Colleen hadn't voiced the offer first.

"Everybody needs a little kindness from time to time. It seemed he was a bit overdue for some." She turned and pulled Abby into her arms for a brief hug. "I'd best be getting some of this stuff down there. He'll be back in no time at the rate he was going." She asked some of the crew to help her, and within a few minutes, their four chests and assorted boxes were stacked on the pier. As the last box was stacked neatly, the sound of horse hooves could be heard on the wooden planks. Colleen looked up to see Tom waving from where he sat beside the driver of a wagon large enough to easily accommodate their luggage and themselves. Tom was leaping from the seat almost before the wagon came to a stop, and he and Colleen loaded everything so there was a space for him in the back. Colleen and Abby would ride up front with the driver.

Charles hurried down the gangplank with a small package in his hands. He was breathless by the time he reached the trio by the side of the wagon. "I was afraid you'd have left before I got a chance to give you this," he gasped as he handed the box to Abby.

"Oh, Father, we wouldn't leave without saying goodbye."

"Be that as it may. You're an impatient woman, Colleen."

"Father, I'm a man here," she spoke softly so only he could hear, and she looked to where the driver stood a few feet away from the wagon. It did not appear he heard what her father said.

"Sorry ... Charles. It will take some getting used to, I fear." He turned to Abby with a smile and said, "Open it, dear."

"It's for me? Oh thank you, Father." Abby had tried many titles to call Charles during the trip, but the only thing that fit for her was father, so that's how she addressed him. Abby tore the paper off the package to reveal a small gold box inlaid with jewels. She gasped as she looked at it, unable to speak.

"Open the box," Charles said, grinning from ear to ear.

"There's more than just the box? But this is beautiful just—oh!" The purple velvet-lined box contained a sapphire pendant, as well as a chain with a matching sapphire in a teardrop shape. The stones were almost a perfect match for Colleen's eye color. Abby's eyes filled with tears as she threw her arms around Charles's neck and hugged him tightly. "Oh, Father, this is the most beautiful thing I've ever seen .... Well, except for Charles," she said with a wink in Colleen's direction.

Colleen watched the interaction between the two people she

loved most in the world, and her heart swelled with happiness. She had not seen the box or its contents since shortly after her mother died. It was a gift to Betsy Ann from her father. Colleen wondered what became of it when her father left but believed he must have disposed of it because of the painful reminder. Obviously, he was not able to part with it, and Colleen was certain he would not have given her such a feminine item. But Abby loved such things, and Colleen knew she would treasure this gift always.

"It belonged to Charles's mother," Charles said, then placed a kiss on Abby's forehead. "It didn't seem like something Charles would appreciate, but I knew you would. Sorry for not giving it to you sooner, but I couldn't get into the chest where it was stored until all your things were removed."

"And I'm sorry we displaced you from your cabin for so long. I'm sure you can't wait to have your own space again."

"I sacrificed it gladly for the pleasure of having you on board," Charles said gallantly, bowing to his daughter-in-law.

"Are ye planning on hanging about here all day?" The driver was tapping his foot a bit impatiently, but since none of them appeared to notice, he decided to hurry things along.

"Hold your horses," Colleen said with a chuckle. She realized she always wanted to say that, but never had the opportunity before now. She walked to her father's side and held out her hand to give his a shake. He took the hand but then pulled her into a hug.

"Fathers can hug their sons, too, you know," he whispered into her ear.

"I guess they can." She hugged him back, then pulled away to look into his face. "We'll see you when you're finished unloading your cargo in Hartlepool, Father. And remember, if you need me to sail with you in the future, I'll be happy to do that. Whenever you feel you have had enough of the sea, come and live with us here. I'll miss you."

"It's time for you now, Col," he said softly. "Make your own life with that lovely woman. I'll get back here as often as I can."

"Wait! Wait!" They all turned to see James Henry running down the gangplank as fast as his old stubby legs would take him.

In one hand, he held a scabbard and sword and in the other, a finely tooled leather belt and frog. He skidded to a stop in front of Colleen and held out both hands to her.

She took the items reverently; she knew they were a treasure to him, and it touched her that he wanted her to have them. He told her once the story of how his father had performed a service for the king, and in return, the king had given him the jewel-encrusted blade. "Mr. Henry, I can't take this," Colleen said. Tears threatened to fall, and she took a deep breath and willed them not to.

"They're of no use to me, Col. I want ye to have them. It will make me proud to think of ye wearing them. And maybe from time to time, ye'll think of me when you do."

Colleen fitted the belt around her waist and hung the scabbard within the frog. After a few adjustments, it hung perfectly within reach of her hand. "I'll think of you all the time, Mr. Henry. You're a dear man and a great friend."

"Can we be done now with all this yammering?" the driver said in a tone bordering on churlish. "I have other stops to make, and you're putting me behind time."

Colleen turned toward him, her eyes blazing. "Have a care, sir! You are in the company of the daughter of Lord Hume, and I'll thank you to keep a civil tongue. We're nearly ready to go. Please give us the courtesy of a few moments to say farewell to our family."

The driver scuttled over to the side of the wagon farthest from the group without making further complaint.

"Abby, give your father-in-law a hug," Charles said, opening his arms. Abby threw herself into his arms again and kissed him on the cheek.

"I'll treasure this gift always, Father. I'm so honored that you wished to share your beloved Betsy Ann with me. I love you."

"I love you, too. And you're the treasure, dear. Please take good care of my son. I'm counting on you." He turned to Colleen and grasped her hand, shaking it firmly. "And if I hear you've harmed a hair on this little lady's head, you'll live to regret it."

Colleen laughed. "You haven't a worry, Father. Now we need

to get going before the driver has apoplexy. See you in a fortnight."
She climbed aboard the wagon beside the driver and held her hand
down to help Abby up. Tom stood below with his hands around
her waist to steady her, and she dropped gracefully into the seat
next to Colleen. Tom scrambled into the back and knocked on the
back of the seat to let the driver know he was ready, and they set
off for Edinburgh and the Hume ancestral home.

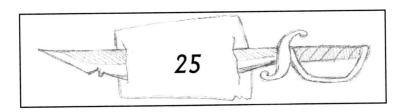

Even though Abby had described her home in great detail, Colleen was not quite prepared for how very large it was. She tried to count all the turrets and towers as they approached but lost count when they made some winding turns and realized she was counting the same ones more than once. Moldering was not the proper word, but there was no question much work was needed on the place. Lord Hume left a small staff to tend to the home and grounds while they were gone, so the outward appearance was adequate, but upon closer inspection, she could see that there were many stones perched in their place by willpower alone.

Colleen was about to assist Abby down from the wagon when the front door opened and a man and three women bustled out to greet them. Lord Hume told Colleen he had dispatched a letter to his overseer to let him know Abby was returning with her new husband and to get the place as presentable as possible before they arrived. The man reached them first, and after bowing first to Abby, then to Colleen, he held out his hand for Abby and said, "Allow me, my lady."

As soon as Abby's feet touched the ground, she launched herself into the old man's arms. "You've gotten older, Mr. McEwan. I almost didn't recognize you."

"Aye, that I have, lass. And ye've grown into a fair beautiful woman. That tropical sun agrees with ye."

The two women reached the wagon by then, and both curtsied to Abby and Colleen. The elder of the two took Abby's hand in hers and patted it softly, smiling to reveal numerous gaps in her teeth. "Mrs. McEwan, I've been looking forward to your cooking ever since I knew we were coming home."

"I can see ye've not been eating well since ye left. Nae worry, lass, I'll fatten ye up." She turned to look Colleen up and down and nodded seriously before adding, "Yer husband could do with a stone himself, I'll warrant."

"Oh, yes, allow me to introduce my husband. This is Charles Edwards the second, son of Charles Edwards, the privateer out of Hartlepool." She took Colleen's hand in hers and sidled closer to her. "Singlehandedly, he saved me from pirates and blew up their ship." Both McEwans and the young maid standing behind them gasped, the younger one clutching at her breast as if in fright. "Don't worry, Bridie. They didn't touch a hair on my head before Charles rescued me. I'll tell you the whole story over tea."

Colleen sighed as the cloth binding her breasts dropped to the floor. During the voyage, she returned to the way she used to dress, which meant loose-fitting sailor's garb and no bindings. But she vowed she would appear as a proper English gentleman when they returned to Scotland, so while sitting at anchor in Georgetown, South Carolina, she commissioned a tailor to make her some clothing suitable for a man of means. Her sea-going apparel would remain on board the *Betsy Ann*. She knew of course that Abby would have a maid to assist her with dressing and undressing but did not realize the same courtesy would be extended to her. She politely declined the butler's offer to help her undress, but from the way he looked at her, she knew she would have to contrive a believable explanation for why she would dress herself. Perhaps she could say Abby was her dresser, and she wanted no other. Yes, that sounded plausible. The only place she could now be free to be herself would be in their rooms.

"What was that sigh about?" Abby said, kissing her lightly on the shoulder.

"Nothing really, just thinking about how different things are going to be. I know the butler means well, but I can't have him undressing me."

"Oh my, I forgot about that. Of course not. Tell him I'll take care of that chore." She curved her lips in a very suggestive smile. "I rather fancy undressing you."

Colleen laughed. "I already planned to tell him exactly that. And I fancy undressing you. Do you suppose we can dismiss your maid as well?" Abby was already in her nightgown, the fire was blazing in the fireplace, and the bedclothes were turned down.

"Perhaps. You should undress me now ... to show me how well you're qualified for the job."

"A pleasure, my lady." Colleen unfastened the buttons on the gown until it was loose enough to pull over her head, and with a flourish, she yanked the garment off, tossing it to the floor. "I'm sure I can do it even faster with practice," she said huskily, her eyes devouring the exposed skin of her wife.

Abby laughed and said, "Ah, you don't need to be faster ... unless you have teased me first by flaunting your bare breasts in my face." Colleen wiggled her eyebrows and winked lasciviously while cupping her breasts. "Which you have done, so I guess a little speed is not a bad idea. Shall I show you how fast I can remove your clothes, husband?"

At Colleen's nod, Abby's hands flew to the buttons of the trousers. She pulled so hard that two of them flew off and clattered on the floor across the room. "I'll sew them back on, no worry. Now step out of these, please."

Colleen did as she was bid, and the two women stood inches apart, about to make love for the first time in a bed that did not bob up and down on water. Colleen leaned down to brush her lips over Abby's, and Abby draped her arms over Colleen's shoulders. "Take me to bed," Abby whispered in her ear, and without hesitation, Colleen scooped her up and carried her to the bed, laying her down, then crawling up beside her.

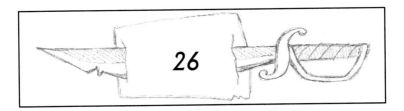

26

Two years later

The sound of an infant wailing with the first intake of breath woke Colleen from where she dozed in a chair. Abby was already on her feet and moving toward the door when the midwife came out with the tiny crying creature in her hands. The expression on her face was not what one would expect when one assisted in the birth of what appeared to be a normal healthy boy.

"What is it? What's wrong?" Abby asked. She knew Bridie went into labor earlier than she should have and had been struggling with the birth for the better part of two days.

"It's the mum, my lady. This little one battered her, and no mistake. I couldn't stop the bleeding after he was born, and the poor wee thing just didn't have the strength to survive. I'm sorry I was nae able to save her. What d'ye want me to do with the wee bairn?"

It was fortunate that Colleen had risen from her seat and was standing beside Abby when she heard that Bridie died, for Abby's knees gave out and she would have collapsed but for Colleen's arms supporting her. Colleen led Abby to a chair and set her down, concerned at the pallor of her skin.

Abby shook her head as if to try to grasp what had just happened, and she whispered, "Aw, Bridie, no," as tears leaked down her cheeks. She looked down at Colleen who was kneeling at her feet, holding her hand. "She was like a sister to me, Charles. Her mother was our cook when I was a child. We were nearly the same age and used to sneak out to play together when our mothers were busy. My mother would have been scandalized to know I was playing tea time with a servant. I—I loved her."

Colleen knelt down in front of Abby and took both her hands in her own. "I know you did, and I could see she loved you, too." Colleen stood and turned to where the midwife stood with the baby clutched to her bosom. "May I hold the baby, Mrs. Beaton?"

"Of course, sir. But mind your clothes, they're a bit leaky at this age." She held out the tiny bundle, and Colleen reached to accept him. Mrs. Beaton clucked and shook her head. "Put your hand behind his head, sir, he's a fragile creature." Colleen did as she asked and held the infant against her chest, her hand firmly behind his head.

Colleen walked to where Abby sat and with every step found herself falling in love with the helpless baby. She never thought of herself in terms of motherhood; it simply did not fit with her idea of what her life would be. But with Abby by her side, raising a child together did not seem so daunting. She knew from what Abby told her shortly after they arrived in Scotland, that Bridie was orphaned at an early age. Lord Hume was unable to locate any other relatives, so she remained in their care and became Abby's chambermaid. "Would you like to hold him, Abby?"

Abby blinked and drew a deep breath, willing the tears to stop flowing. She did not want this baby's first sight of her to be with a tear-streaked face. When Colleen laid him in the crook of her arms, the infant sighed and relaxed against her breast, apparently asleep. She touched his face with her fingers and found the skin almost too soft to be real. "Oh, Charles, what a beautiful being he is." She leaned down and kissed his forehead, smelling the clean scent of one who has not been marred by time and circumstance.

"Indeed, he is," Colleen hastened to agree, hoping Abby would reach the same conclusion about his fate as she had.

"He has no other family," Abby said, knowing the man who had robbed Bridie of her virginity and left her with child was no more a father than he was a gentleman. "We can raise him as our own, can't we, dear?" Colleen nodded enthusiastically. "It's settled then." She turned to where Mrs. Beaton stood, undoubtedly expecting her to hand the infant over to her care. Instead she said, "Mrs. Beaton, I would be most grateful if you would not tell anyone about his unfortunate beginnings. Let them think it was I who gave birth to the lad. Will you do that for me?"

"Of course, my lady. 'Tis the best thing for the bairn. How horrible he would feel to learn he was the cause of his mother's death. You may rely on my discretion, my lady."

"I appreciate that. Will you ask Mr. McEwan to come up here? I need to make arrangements to bury Bridie."

"Yes, my lady." She curtsied and left the room, and Colleen drew a chair up to sit beside Abby.

"He's so little," Colleen whispered, taking his fragile hand and holding it between two fingers. His own tiny fingers curled around hers, and her heart was lost to the infant from that moment.

Abby cuddled the small bundle close to her breast, and the baby turned toward her as if seeking something. Not sure what to do, Abby looked at Colleen.

"He's hungry," she said, grinning at the infant rooting around Abby's breast, a most favorite spot of her own. "I'll see about getting him some milk. My mother gave sugared goat's milk to Thomas for weeks after he was born because she could not make enough milk for the little pig." She walked to the door, then turned back to see Abby leaning down and kissing the baby's forehead. It was obvious Abby was as smitten by the wee mite as she was.

Abby caught Colleen looking at her and the baby and smiled. "I think we should name him John Charles, after both our fathers. We could call him Johnny." She kissed the tip of the infant's nose and looked back at Colleen. "How does that sound?"

"Sounds like we have a son named Johnny."

As the days grew warmer, Abby and Colleen made it a practice to take Johnny out to nap in the sun while Abby painted and Colleen tended to chores about the place. At noon, they would both stop what they were doing and have tea, and when Johnny woke up, Colleen would tend to him while Abby painted. In the two years since they had lived in Scotland, Abby had made quite a name for herself as a painter. Her work was hanging on walls from York to London, and she could name her price in Edinburgh. The income from her work allowed them to make great headway in effecting repairs to the manor house, and Colleen involved herself with the workmen to ensure everything was done to her satisfaction. Lord and Lady Hume would be most pleased with the progress when they returned from Nassau, which would be very soon.

On one particularly sunny day, Abby set up her easel in the shade of a tree to escape the heat. Johnny was in his basket by her feet, and after a hearty meal, Colleen was lounging on the ground near the base of the tree dozing. When Johnny made little whimpering noises, Colleen picked him up and laid back down where she was with the baby on her chest. He settled back down immediately, and Colleen once again fell asleep. Abby set aside the painting she was working on when she saw the beautiful vision that was her husband and son. Taking up a piece of parchment, she quickly sketched the two people she loved most in the world, intending to one day use the sketch to create a painting. It would be a surprise for Colleen, perhaps for her birthday.

Abby barely finished the sketch when she heard the sound of a wagon approaching. The noise roused Colleen, as well, and she sat up with Johnny clutched tightly in her arms. Abby hid the sketch behind her painting and covered the easel with an oil-soaked cloth to keep it from drying out. "Were you expecting anyone?" she asked Colleen.

"Not today. The stonemason is coming out tomorrow. Perhaps it's Lord and Lady Hume. I think we should go up to the house and see."

"Oh! Of course, that's who it must be." She helped Colleen to her feet, then gathered her painting supplies. "Can you manage the baby, as well as my paint box? I can handle the easel by myself."

"Certainly, just give me a moment to tuck him in his basket." She put Johnny in his bed, and after tucking it under one arm, she took hold of the handle of the paint box in the other hand and set off for the house. Abby followed behind with the easel held carefully to avoid smudging the paint.

The wagon had just come to a stop near the front door by the time they reached the manor house. Indeed, Lord and Lady Hume were disembarking from the wagon when they arrived, and Colleen was pleased to see that her father accompanied them. The looks on all of their faces when they saw the tiny hands waving from the basket Colleen carried made her glad they had decided to keep the news of the baby from them until they were there to see him in person.

"Och, is that what I think it is?" Emelia shouted in a decidedly unlady-like tone as she rushed to Colleen's side to see what the basket contained.

Colleen beamed and said, "If you think it's a baby, then yes, it is what you think it is. Or rather he is what you think. I'm proud to introduce you to your grandson, John Charles Edwards." Colleen noticed the look her father gave her, which clearly said he wondered how they'd managed this miracle. She walked to his side and hugged him, whispering in his ear as she did, "I'll tell you all about it later."

"May I hold him?" Emelia gushed, and when Abby nodded, she picked the baby up, holding him at arm's length to get a look at him. "Och, he's the most beautiful baby I've seen since Abigail. He has your lovely blue eyes, Charles." Johnny chose that moment to soil his diaper, making Emelia glad she had not immediately clutched him to her bosom as she'd planned.

"I'll take him, Mother," Abby said, reaching out for him.

"So long as I get him back as soon as he's cleaned up." Emelia followed Abby as she made her way to the house, where the wet nurse was already standing waiting for the baby. Abby transferred the odiferous bundle into her arms, and both women watched as the nurse took him inside. Emelia turned Abby around to face her and hugged her more tightly than Abby could ever remember. "Thank you, dear. I have to tell you, I thought I would not live to see any grandchildren, but now I feel blessed indeed. You've made an old woman very happy."

"Pooh, Mother, you are not old," she said as she pulled back from her mother's embrace. But in truth, she could see lines etched in her mother's face that were not there when she left Nassau. She fought back a stab of guilt for having left her there, but the look on Emelia's face when Margaret, the wet nurse, brought Johnny back wiped away any remorse she might have felt.

Abby nodded to Margaret to give the baby to her mother, and she complied. Turning to Abby, Margaret said, "I tried to nurse him, but he was fussy and not interested. I think perhaps he senses something is different and wants to be in on it."

Emelia rocked the infant in her arms, smiling as he gurgled and laughed at her. "He likes me," she said happily. "But why are you not nursing him? A baby needs its mother."

Abby was prepared with the story she and Colleen had come up with for why she was not nursing the baby herself. Leaning closer to her mother so the men wouldn't hear, she said, "I was not producing enough milk for him, so we hired Margaret. And now he prefers her milk to mine, so I stopped even trying, and my milk has dried up."

"Oh. Well, so long as he is getting mother's milk. I've heard so many sad stories about babies dying...."

Abby jumped in before Emelia could continue. Margaret was still within reach of her voice, and her own baby had died shortly before she came to live with them and nurse Johnny; the poor woman did not need a reminder of her loss. "He's healthy and vital, Mother. I expect he'll be talking in full sentences and running about before we know it. You can tell by the look in his eyes that he has a bright mind in that pretty little head of his."

"Are we going to stand about out here all day, or can we go in the house and have tea like civilized people?" Lord John complained, but his voice was light, and he winked at Abby as he said it.

Abby launched herself into his arms and hugged him tightly. "I've missed you, Father. And, yes, we're going to have tea. I had Mrs. McEwan prepare something special in anticipation of your arrival, but since we had no idea when that might be, we were forced to eat it ourselves." She laughed at the expression of dismay on his face. "Don't worry, I'm sure she can throw something suitable together in short order." Abby gestured for them all to go inside and fell into step beside her mother as the older woman climbed the stairs.

Colleen took her father aside before he followed the others and explained to him what had happened with Bridie and the baby. He listened intently, then said, "It's a shame about the young woman, but a blessing for the child that he was born here where there are two people who love him very much. I'm honored to have him in the family, Col."

"Thank you, Dad. That means more to me than I can say. Come, let's go get something to eat before Lord Hume consumes it all."

After tea, they retired to the parlor, where Lord Hume and Charles spoke of the price of spices and such from India, as the women fussed over the baby. Colleen tried to take an interest in the men's conversation, but her eyes were constantly being drawn to Abby and their baby. She excused herself and went to join Abby on the settee. Abby smiled and patted Colleen's hand, happy to have her there with her. It seemed the two of them never tired of watching Johnny, despite the fact that, at only two months, he did almost nothing but sleep.

"Oh, Abby, I nearly forgot, I have a parcel here for you," Lord Hume said, drawing a parchment and a wrapped package from inside his coat. "Your mother said it's from the man who made your wedding dress. We would have forwarded it on to you long ago, but he insisted we bring it to you personally when we returned home."

Abby could not imagine what Pierre could possibly have to say to her, but she walked to where her father sat and took the letter from him. Opening it up, she read:

My Dear Mrs. Edwards,

I thought you would like to know that the mutual friends we discussed have visited me here and are none the worse for wear since the sinking of the *William*.

I talked with them myself and told them about your wedding. They said to give you their congratulations. And Mary particularly asked me to pass along her thanks to you, and to tell you she has included a special gift for you. She seemed to think you would know what that means and suggested you not open the parcel in mixed company.

I wish you and your husband the best of luck in your marriage. Please remember me to your mother and make sure she tells all her friends to come to Port Royal for the most fabulous gowns to be had in the Caribbean.

Yours,

Pierre

Abby chuckled as she handed the letter to Colleen and tucked the parcel unopened in a pocket of her apron. Colleen read the letter, and with a wink to Abby, she folded it and handed it back. She mouthed the words "special gift?" and raised her eyebrows in question. Abby made a gesture that she hoped Colleen would interpret as meaning "I'll show you later."

Emelia looked up from the basket, where Johnny was fast asleep, long enough to ask, "What on earth did the dressmaker have to say, dear?"

"Oh nothing, Mother. He asked me to tell you to send your friends to him for gowns and sent his congratulations to Charles and me on our marriage. He also sent us a small personal wedding gift."

"Well, it's rather a long way for my friends to go for gowns," Emelia said off-handedly, her attention once again immersed in the baby.

"A long way indeed," Abby said, dropping down beside Colleen.

About the Author

Vada Foster is an author, actor and playwright. She lives in southern California with a collection of Shih-Tzu's and a couple of cats, one twin sister and a partner whom she had to go to Florida to find. She enjoys traveling and discovering new places, which she is doing a lot of since she met Gypsy.

Your comments are welcome. Contact the author at: Vada@QueenGypsy.com

You can purchase other Intaglio
Publications books online at
www.bellabooks.com, www.scp-inc.biz, or at
your local book store.

Published by
Intaglio Publications
Walker, LA

Visit us on the web
www.intagliopub.com

Printed in the United States
122838LV00001B/88-93/P

9 781933 113890